The Anger That Grew Me

The Anger That Grew Me

The ANGER That Grew Me

A Memoir of Faith, Trauma, and Transformation

Yolanda L. Washington-Pompey

Dedication

To the mother I barely knew and the father I knew only for a moment—thank you for giving me life. I hope to see you in heaven, to understand your stories, and to ask forgiveness for seeing only my own. I love you both.

To my grandmother—after Jesus and my son, you are the most incredible love my mind can hold. Jesus saved my soul, but you guided me to Him, while carrying me through your own pain.

To my husband and son—my gifts from God—thank you for showing me life beyond my childhood. I love you and thank you for being my family.

To my sisters and brother, thank you for walking this path with me. Not by choice, but by God's plan. Through the pain and the anger, we witnessed His love. I love you all.

Prayer:

Father, I thank You for loving me in ways mankind cannot always recognize as love—through Your sovereignty, grace, mercy, and compassion.

Your love is beyond understanding, and that is why I write this book: to give You glory and remind others that Your will is their becoming.

Help us trust not in our feelings, but in Your Word.

Amen.

Becoming Was Always the Plan
Adult reflection

I didn't know an emotion could raise a child.
But introduce it early, feed it often, and it becomes the parent.

Some children are raised by fear—its voice whispering rules, sounding alarms, teaching caution until it echoes in every thought.

Others by anger—sharp, explosive, sometimes just, sometimes cruel, its lessons carved deep into memory.
Love can raise you too—steady and gentle, or fierce in its demand for loyalty.
To be raised by an emotion is to learn its language before you ever know your own.

Like me, I learned anger before I ever learned to speak.
It held my hand and tucked me in at night when Momma couldn't. When death took her, anger stayed.

It whispered that I didn't need anyone.
That being strong meant never needing to cry.
And I believed it—because anger was faithful when people weren't. But this story isn't mine alone.

It's for every child who grew up trying to fill the empty spaces left by their parents.

For every adult still making peace with the child they once were. For every one of us who was seen—but for all the wrong reasons—and for the person we became when we learned God never left us.

I was that girl—torn between faith and fury, between believing God loved me and wondering why He let life hurt so bad.

I built walls to feel safe, acted out to feel seen, mistaking control for power and rebellion for freedom. But God, like He did with Job, allowed the trial— not to destroy me, but to reveal Himself in it.

Over time, I began to see that anger wasn't the only thing growing in me. Love was there too—quiet, patient, waiting its turn.

This is that story—of a girl Detroit tried to break, yet Jesus chose to save.

From Sirens to Silence
Age 5 — The Day Sirens Took My Mother and Gave Me Anger

Have you ever had a memory you're not sure is real—like something imagined, or a story someone else planted in your mind?

That's how August 1977 feels to me. I think it was August.

I was still small.

What I remember is standing outside, tears streaking dirty down my cheeks because I'd wiped my eyes with muddy hands—fingers caked from playing in puddles all morning, elbow-deep in thick, sticky mud.

The mud was everywhere that summer. It pooled in the low spots by the curb where the concrete had cracked and buckled, and the rainwater settled and wouldn't drain. I learned to find the best mud—not too watery, not too dry—the kind that held its shape when you squeezed it, cool and alive between your fingers.

Momma told me to go outside and play. She always did when "Uncle" came over—whichever uncle it was that week. I knew the routine by then. The way her voice went tight and hurried. "Hoochy, baby, go on outside

now. Go play. Momma needs some grown-up time."
Grown-up time meant the door closed. The curtains
drawn. The TV turned up loud enough to drown out
whatever sounds came from inside.

It meant cigarette smoke seeping through the screen
door.

It meant I wasn't wanted inside my own home.

So, I played in the mud. I made castles that collapsed. I
drew pictures in the wet dirt with sticks. I watched ants
haul crumbs three times their size, amazed that
something so small could carry so much. The warm
summer air clung to my skin, sticky and thick. Other kids
played down the block—I heard their shouts, the slap of
a jump rope against pavement, someone's transistor
radio crackling out Stevie Wonder. But I stayed close to
657, near our doorstep, because Momma said not to
wander far.

I was always waiting.

Waiting to be called back in.

Waiting to be wanted again.

Then came the sirens.

Ambulances were common in our neighborhood, so sirens usually didn't catch me off guard. People got shot, fights broke out—day after day, I saw it all unfold right in front of me.

Yet that day, the sirens sounded different. They didn't rush past—they stopped. Fast. Loud. Tires screeching right outside our door.

That day, the siren was personal.

My little heart thumped with something I couldn't name—somewhere between horror and hope. The sound sliced through the block, and my body tensed as fear rose, uninvited. I didn't know why, but in that moment, everything slowed. The world went quiet, as if someone had found the remote to my heartbeat and pressed pause—leaving only the soft squelch of mud beneath my palms. I didn't know it then, but noise could brand itself into a child's memory, the way grief teaches your ears to remember what your heart can't forget.

I stood up. My legs felt shaky, unsteady. Mud dripped from my hands onto my bare knees, leaving dark streaks down my ashy skin. The sun beat down on the back of my neck, but I felt cold.

The ambulance doors flew open. White uniforms moved fast and purposefully. A stretcher rattled as they pulled it out, metal legs unfolding with a mechanical click-click-click.

They were going into my house.

My house

Momma!

I caught a glimpse of her when the paramedics rushed inside.

Momma was still.

Not the kind of stillness that comes from sleeping—I knew what her sleep looked like, with its gentle inhale, exhale, and tiny movements of dreams. Almost rhythmic, as if a song was always playing in her mind as she breathed in and out. This was a different stillness, without rhythm. I saw "Uncle" George standing over her.

My emotions tore at each other. I looked at him—furious one minute, wailing the next. Fear, confusion, rage, grief—spilling out of me like a newborn's scream after that first gasp of air, that slap into life, a pain nobody asked for.

My small fists curled tight. I was mad. Scared. Lost.

But most of all, I didn't even know who I was angry at.

Was it George—after that quick glimpse of the rubber strap looped in his hand before the door shut? Was it God—for not helping her? The neighborhood— for never releasing her from the streets? Angry at *her*—for choosing them? Or at *me*—for not saying, *"Momma, don't leave me outside,"* and staying quiet instead?

Or all of them?

In that silence, something inside me broke. That day, hope slipped away—not as loud as the sirens, but as quiet as my own voice. And anger moved in, taking up the space where Shanky once was.

The front door of our house—657 Eliot—is burned into my memory. The stenciled white numbers on the mailbox glared out against the chipped paint. The door stood wide open, the screen propped by the little silver wedge we only used when there were too many groceries or a piece of furniture to drag inside.

Then came the bodies—strangers rushing in and out. The smell of cigarettes and sweat, the sour liquor—it stung my nostrils. Pee-yew!

Faces surrounded me—some I think I knew, most I didn't. Police who didn't smile pushed me aside.

"Move out of the way, little girl."

I caught my breath and looked up like a scared kitten—a muddy kitten—hoping somebody would ask me what was wrong.

Nope.

Nobody did.

I wanted to scream. I wanted to grab someone's leg and hold on until they paid attention. But my voice had disappeared somewhere deep inside, swallowed by the walnut-sized lump in my throat.

I tried to move closer to the door, but a police officer's thick arm blocked my path like a gate. His badge caught the sunlight and flashed in my eyes. He smelled like coffee and aftershave. He didn't look at me—his eyes were fixed on something inside the house, something I couldn't see.

"Stay back, sweetheart," he said, but his voice was flat and automatic—the way you'd tell a dog to sit.

I wasn't a person to him. Just an obstacle. Just another project kid in the way.

Then my Auntie's sharp voice cut through the noise.

Granddad's tired face followed, half-hidden behind his handkerchief.

I heard that trumpet-blow sound of him wiping his nose—the wet sound that meant he'd been crying.

Granddad never cried.
Not when his girlfriend got sick.
Not even when somebody broke into his house and took his TV, but he was crying, and that scared me more than the sirens, more than the ambulance, more than George.

I tried to peek past my big uncle's frame filling the kitchen doorway, my head bobbing up and down like Whac-A-Mole, slipping between the officer's arm and Unk's body when I could.
That's when I spotted someone else, I knew—
Uncle Evan, in his wheelchair.

He was my favorite. He lived just down the street. He played his guitar and keyboard and sang to us, and it made us feel less lonely.

He babysat us and never made us uneasy—unlike some of the other "uncles" who drifted in and out of Momma's life. Any man who walked through our door was an uncle—at least that's what they called themselves.

Uncle Evan's face looked gray. He gripped the armrests so tightly that his knuckles turned to white marbles under his dark skin. His mouth moved, but no sound came, like he was praying or just trying not to fall apart.

Voices rose to shouts—I pressed my hands over my ears, forgetting about the mud until I felt the grit against my temples. The air felt crowded and unsettled, scared and hopeless. The ambulance people moved quickly, like it was just another day.

I wanted to ask what was happening, but my throat hurt as if a walnut was stuck somewhere deep inside, leaving just enough room to breathe.

They carried my Momma's body out.

Time fractured!

Everything moved in slow motion and fast-forward at once. The stretcher wheels caught on the threshold. Someone cursed.

They adjusted, lifted, and maneuvered through the doorway with practiced efficiency.

The ambulance doors gaped open like a hungry mouth waiting for a spoonful.

Neighbors whispered behind cupped hands. Police scribbled in their little notebooks, their eyes sliding past me—past my petite frame—as if I were a ghost. I watched the paramedics move with steady calm around the white-sheeted figure on the stretcher—the one the ambulance was preparing to swallow.

The sheet was pristine, too clean for something so wrong. As they lifted the stretcher, a corner snagged on the ambulance doorframe and peeled back, revealing a flash of familiar curly black hair and half a face—eyes open, unblinking.

"Momma," I whispered, the word barely more than a breath.

Her eyes were open, empty. Looking at nothing. Looking through everything. Looking past me as if I were already gone—as if I'd never been there at all.

I wanted her to blink. To turn her head. To see me standing there, covered in mud and tears, and say, "Hoochy, baby, why you crying? Momma's right here."

But she didn't move. Didn't blink. Didn't breathe.

The paramedic—a white woman with her hair pulled tight—tucked the sheet back over Momma's face with quick, efficient motions. Not gentle. Not cruel. Just... done. Like covering leftovers for the refrigerator.

No one looked at her. Not the cops. Not the paramedics.

When the ambulance doors slammed shut, the sound was finality itself. The sirens stayed silent—no wailing. No red lights spun with urgency. Only the quiet rumble of an engine carrying away everything that mattered, while my little body just stood and watched.

Someone—I don't know who—picked me up. My body dangled, too stunned to fight, too angry to cry. Flakes of mud trailed behind me, falling from my hands and shoes as they carried me. The arms didn't pause or explain.

I remember the smell—Old Spice and cigarettes. Strong arms, not comforting. Just functional. Moving me from point A to point B, like a package.

My head bounced against their shoulder. The world tilted. I watched 657 Eliot grow smaller and smaller behind us—the door still open, the screen door still propped, the mailbox numbers glaring white against rust.

So, I focused on the building's number as it came toward me: **662.**

They say home is where the heart is,
but what if your heart stayed behind
in the mud outside 657?
What if home became the place
you were carried to—
not chosen,
just dropped,
like a letter to the wrong address?
Grief doesn't knock.
It kicks the door in.
It covers faces with white sheets.
It takes your mother
and leaves you with questions
no one will answer.
At five years old,
I learned that love leaves.
That sirens mean loss.

That mud keeps the prints of your small hands long after you're gone.

The sirens were loud, but not louder than the voice in my head. Anger doesn't shout — it hisses. It told me she chose them over me.

Grandma Pearl

THE WOMAN WHO SAVED US WITH STRENGTH, NOT SOFTNESS

662 Eliot.

Grandma Pearl's house. My Momma's momma.

Even now, saying her name brings her back—sharp and soft all at once.

Pearl's voice was its own kind of siren—sharp enough to scatter trouble, strong enough to call us home.

I remember one morning in her bright, warm kitchen, linoleum floors worn into a patchwork—faded yellow and brown squares, some cracked, some curling at the edges where the glue had given up. We crowded around the heavy ivory-topped table, eating cornflakes—soggy flakes drowning in milk, buried under too much sugar. When I scooped up the slimy banana slices floating on top, the grainy sugar scraped the spoon. The flakes clung to it, then slipped away before reaching my mouth. I hated them, especially when the smell of real food drifted through, taunting me with what I couldn't have yet.

No one made fresh dough biscuits like Grandma Pearl. She'd roll out the dough on that same ivory table, dusting it with flour that puffed up like little clouds.

She'd cut them with a mayonnaise jar, or an empty food can, each one perfect. Bigger than KFC's, crust flaking just right—soft inside, salty enough to linger on your tongue. Kind of like Popeye's, but with more love and less pretense. And that butter! Not fake stuff. Rich, greasy, real—like Church's. Those biscuits weren't just food; they were comfort you could taste, love made edible.

When Grandma pulled them from the oven, the kitchen filled with warmth that had nothing to do with temperature. She'd split one open while it was still steaming, slather it with butter that melted into golden pools, and hand it to me—never a plate, just my hand.

"Don't burn your tongue, baby," she'd say, but I always did. Too eager. Too hungry for something that smelled so good.

One day, a woman came to Grandma's back door. It was always open on warm mornings, letting a gentle breeze drift through, carrying the smell of somebody's breakfast and the sound of Mr. Henry's radio playing the blues two units down.

"Hey, Pearl-ll!" she called—the way folks dragged that L made it sound like an old man calling from across the yard.

Her name was carried through the neighborhood.

Even folks who passed on the way to church or the liquor store called her name the same way. Pearl was somebody. Not because she had money or status, but because she'd survived when survival wasn't guaranteed. Because she fed people even when her own cabinets were almost bare. Because she spoke the truth, whether you wanted to hear it or not.

"I'm hungry," the woman said. She stood on the back stoop in a housedress two sizes too big, hair wrapped in a scarf, feet bare against the hot concrete.

"I have some eggs," Grandma answered, not looking up from the stove where she was frying something in an iron skillet.

"I don't eat eggs, Pearl-ll."

Pearl turned, spatula in hand, eyebrows raised. "Well, you ain't hungry, then."

The woman sucked her teeth and walked away, muttering something under her breath I couldn't hear. Grandma shook her head and went back to her skillet, unbothered.

That was my grandma—sharp tongue, soft heart.

She'd feed you if you were truly hungry. She'd clothe you if you were naked. But she had no patience for choosy beggars or folks who confused want with need. She'd survived too much to waste anything—not food, not time, and not sympathy for people who weren't ready to help themselves.

When I think back, I see the monkey bars behind Grandma's unit, just across the curb out back. Nickie and I played there every Sunday after church.

After squeezing our feet into too-tight black shiny shoes—the kind that pinched your toes and rubbed blisters on your heels—and sitting through Sunday School where we colored pictures of Jesus with the same five crayons worn down to nubs, we'd run straight to those bars.

Our hands were raw from rust in summer, frozen in winter—and we didn't care, one bit. We'd hang upside down until our faces turned red and our church dresses fell over our heads, revealing our cotton underwear. We'd swing from bar to bar, pretending we were circus performers or superheroes or anything other than project kids in hand-me-down dresses.

"Hoochy-Nickie, get in here!" Grandma would yell from the back door, like we were one person.

Sometimes she'd stand there with her hands on her hips, shaking her head at the sight of us—dresses dirty, shoes scuffed, hair coming loose from the careful plaits she'd woven that morning.

"Y'all go on and tear up everything I get you," she'd mutter, but there was no real anger in it. Just resignation. Just love disguised as annoyance.

Pearl came up out of Arkansas in 1922, when Black folks didn't expect fairness—just prayed for mercy.

Her parents died when she was two. What happened to them was never shared with us. That's how it was back then—some stories stayed buried because digging them up wouldn't change a thing. It wouldn't bring anyone back. It would only make the pain fresh again.

She and her sisters were split up, passed from house to house to whoever could handle another mouth. Some homes were kind. Most weren't. Comfort wasn't something you expected.

She grew up picking cotton under a scorching sun, sharp plants tearing at her fingers, her back bent before she was even a teenager. Complaining didn't change anything—you worked, kept your head down, looked out for your own. Childhood wasn't an option. It was a luxury reserved for people who could afford it, and Pearl's people couldn't. But she had spirit—the kind that comes from knowing the world doesn't owe you anything, and you stand tall anyway. The kind that says, "I'm here, and I matter, whether you recognize it or not."

That's the woman who raised me. Not perfect, not gentle, but steady. Like an oak tree that's weathered every storm and refuses to fall.

Pearl survived the Depression. She told stories of eating flour paste when there was nothing else, of wearing shoes cut from cardboard, of watching grown men cry because they couldn't feed their families.

During World War II, she worked in defense factories—an honest *Rosie the Riveter*.
She assembled plane parts, her hands steady even as her feet swelled and her back ached.

Before that, she'd worked as a maid for white families in Michigan, scrubbing their floors, washing their clothes, raising their children while her own sisters scattered to the wind. She'd smile and say, "Yes, ma'am" and "No, sir" while they called her by her first name and she called them Mr. and Mrs.

She had four kids, three girls and a boy. Shanky was the second girl, my momma. Then came the others, each one carrying pieces of Pearl's strength and Pearl's pain.

The Brewsters

We lived right across the street from Grandma Pearl in the Brewster Projects of Detroit. My Momma's house—657 Eliot—sat diagonally from hers at 662. Back then, I didn't think there was anything different about how we lived. To me, the Brewsters were home—the only home I knew.

The Brewster-Douglass Housing Projects sat downtown near the Chrysler Freeway and Mack Avenue—a place where legends were born: Diana Ross, Mary Wilson, Smokey Robinson, Stevie Wonder, Lily Tomlin, Loni Love, and sports legend Joe Louis.

They were the projects—the kind people wrote songs about, the kind that produced greatness despite—or maybe because of—the struggles.

The red-brick buildings had flat roofs and narrow windows that peered over the street like tired eyes. Every block kept its own rhythm—courtyards, back alleys, grass patches hardened by too many footsteps.

Clotheslines sagged under heavy laundry, white sheets and faded towels flapping like flags of surrender. Rusted fences marked boundaries, not privacy.

The community was tight-knit. We shared our food, clothes, laughs, tears, and struggles. We watched out for each other's kids; anyone's mother or father could whip you for doing wrong, with love and without apology. You didn't dare talk back to Mrs. Johnson or Mr. Carter, even if they weren't your parents, because they'd wear you out and then send you home for your own parents to finish the job.

That's just how it was: the whole neighborhood raised you. The whole neighborhood corrected you. And somehow, despite the poverty, the crime, and the pain, you felt held.

The Brewsters stood like fortresses—six-story buildings of stubborn mortar that had seen everything and refused to crumble. The unit doors were so close you could hold your screen door open and knock on your neighbors at the same time.

I did that plenty and got scolded just as often.

"Hoochy, close that door! You're letting all the flies out!"

"Hoochy, quit banging on folks' doors!"

The Brewsters were noisy. Poor. Drug-infested. Still, they were alive. People were always outside—rain or shine, even in the winter cold. The porches were our couches. Sidewalks were our playgrounds. The courtyards were our living rooms.

We jumped rope until the streetlights came on, chanting rhymes that had been passed down for generations. We played hopscotch on chalk-drawn squares that faded in the rain and were redrawn the next day.

We played Miss Mary Mack—clapping and crossing hands to the rhyme, adding extra beats when the words repeated:

Miss Mary Mack, Mack, Mack

All dressed in black, black, black

With silver buttons, buttons, buttons

All down her back, back, back...

That rhyme still echoes in my head sometimes, taking me back to laughing under a cloudless sky—when missing a clap was my biggest worry.

Meanwhile, the adults played dice on upturned crates. Money changed hands faster than I could follow, voices rising and falling with each roll. They played stickball in the street, using trash cans for bases and a crushed beer can for the ball.

Cars lined the street—some shining with fresh wax, some held together by duct tape and prayer—their doors flung open, Motown blasting:

The Temptations. The Four Tops. Gladys Knight and the Pips. Music was everywhere. It spilled from windows and car speakers. It was the heartbeat of the Brewsters, the soundtrack of survival.

The Brewsters were more than crime and poverty—they were Black culture in motion. Detroit rhythm. Gritty, gifted, golden. We didn't have much, but we had music. We had style—platform shoes and bell-bottoms, afros picked high and proud, wide collars and leather jackets.

We had each other. In the middle of all that noise and need, hope still burned bright enough to light up the block. Our faith outshouted our hunger. It stood taller than our circumstances.

Every Sunday, the choir's voices rose in praise— *Amazing Grace, how sweet the sound*—and their songs spilled into the streets. Folks sang along from their stoops, shouting "Amen!" with the rest, even if they hadn't set foot in a church in months—my grandmother included.

She sang, but Grandma didn't go anymore. She used to—back when she went to Shiloh Baptist, dressed in her Sunday best with her hat pinned just so. But somewhere along the way, she started blaming God, too.

When she stopped going, it wasn't the singing she walked away from. It wasn't the preaching. It was the losses. She'd lost too much—buried too many. Watching too many people, she loved get swallowed by the streets and addiction, by a world that chewed folks up and spit them out without a second thought.

Even so, she made sure we kept going to church. She said it was because Momma was sick and we needed to pray for her. I didn't understand then that the sickness she meant was already more than prayer could fix.

What They Didn't Say

Nobody told me my mother was dead. Not that day. Not the next day. Not even the day after that. Their silence was louder than any siren.

They said she was "sick." They said she "went to the hospital." They said, "the Lord called her home," which didn't make sense, because home was here at 657 Eliot—where her coffee cup still sat on the counter, dried rings at the bottom.

Adults talked in code around me—lowering their voices when I entered a room, switching subjects mid-sentence, as if I couldn't tell.

"Poor baby," someone would whisper.

"She don't understand," someone else would say.

"Probably better that way."

But I did understand. Maybe not in words—not in the way adults understand death, with paperwork, funeral arrangements, and that quiet phrase they used: "putting away."

I understood death the way kids understand loss—something that was here is gone, and no one will say if it's ever coming back.

I understood the hollow feeling in my stomach, the kind that had nothing to do with hunger.

I understood it in the way 657 Eliot stayed empty—the door finally closed, the screen door's little wedge gone.

And I understood it in the way people looked at me now—with pity, with sadness, and with something that felt like fear— as if whatever had taken my mother might be contagious.

So, I learned to read silence—the way Grandma's lips pressed tight when anyone said my mother's name.

When the house got quiet like that, she'd pull me onto her lap—though I was getting too big for that—and rock me while humming the hymns I knew from church:

Precious Lord, take my hand.

Lead me on, let me stand...

She would explain that things would get better. Didn't offer platitudes about heaven or angels or God's plan. She just held me, her chin resting against the top of my head, her body sturdy and warm and there.

In the Brewster Projects, death was a frequent visitor— uninvited but familiar, like a cousin who shows up without calling first. We learned to make room for it the way we made room for everything else: by squeezing closer together, by sharing what little we had, by singing louder than the sirens.

They say it takes a village to raise a child. But what happens when the village is grieving too?

When the elders are tired?

When the mothers are missing?

When the fathers are ghosts?

Who raises the child then?

Living with Grandma wasn't like living with Momma. There were rules at 662. You woke up when Grandma said, "Y'all going to school today?"—as if any of us had a choice. You ate what was put in front of you. You went to church on Sunday whether you felt like it or not. You kept your space clean. You didn't talk back. You didn't slam doors. You didn't bring trouble to her doorstep.

At first, I tested those boundaries the way all children do—pushing to see what would bend, what would break, what would hold.

Grandma didn't bend.

She didn't break.

She held.

On those nights when the dream visited me, I'd wake in the dark and hear Grandma in the kitchen—the soft shuffle of her slippers, the clink of a spoon against a cup—at two or three in the morning. I'd creep to the doorway and watch her at that ivory table, lips moving in silent prayer. She never saw me. Or if she did, she never let on.

I think she was carrying all of us—me, Nickie, Fat-al, Sheritta, her son Unk—and her own grief too. The weight of a neighborhood kept swallowing up its children, dragging them from their homes to the streets, from the streets to the needle. Addiction taking the mothers, the fathers—the families.

I think she was praying, asking God why, or just asking for strength to face another day.

Back then, I didn't know how to thank her—for carrying what I couldn't, for being steady when everything else was chaos. I used to watch ants hauling things three times their size and marvel at how something so small could carry so much. I know now because of her.

I'd slip and call her Momma sometimes, and she'd quickly correct me: "Hoochy, I ain't your momma. I'm

Grandma." Her voice was firm, not unkind. I would walk away in pain, in silence.

And in that silence, anger began to grow.

Becoming 'Hoochy'
THE NAME THAT SHAPED MY SURVIVAL

Yeah, they called me Hoochy. And I loved it.

Because "Yolanda" never felt like me. The name "Yolanda" sounded like it belonged to someone soft. Protected. Someone's precious daughter. Someone who mattered. I wasn't.

The name came with expectations I couldn't meet. Yolanda was the name on my birth certificate, the name teachers called during roll call, the name on report cards and doctor's forms. But it never fit right. Like wearing someone else's shoes—technically my size, but shaped to a different foot.

Growing up, if somebody called out "Yolanda," I wouldn't even look up. That name belonged to a girl who got bedtime stories at night, hugs and kisses in the morning—someone who had a family, a mom, and a dad.

Well, there are two versions of how I got the nickname "Hoochy"—with a Y, not an ie.

And that Y made all the difference. It wasn't soft. It wasn't sweet. Famine. It wasn't something you gave a child you planned to protect.

"Hoochie" with an "ie" at the end sounded like a term of endearment—cute, playful, loving. But "Hoochy" with a "Y"? That was something else. Harder. Rougher. Masculine. More street.

It was a label—slapped on the girl in the background— the one nobody picked up to hug, never good enough to be seen. "Hoochy" became mine.

Not chosen, but claimed—two misfits meeting in a name nobody else wanted.

We were both perfectly imperfect, stitched together by what others discarded. The Bible says, "He knew you in your mother's womb." Sometimes, I wonder if God chose my nickname Himself, already carving out a path for me. This one—she's not meant for easy; she's meant for hard. Angry, unruly, rule-breaker, dangerous enough to keep her in trouble so she'll run to Me. Right from the start.

Even my name was a joke I didn't get.

There are two stories about how I got it. Nobody ever bothered to pick one and stick with it. They just told whichever version felt funnier that day.

The first story: I was named after hooch—liquor—because, as a baby, I looked drunk.

Wobbly. Glassy-eyed. A little tipsy toddler.

That's how my momma explained it. Said I reminded her of somebody who had one too many and was still trying to stand up straight. "Like a little hooch," she'd say, laughing. "Girl can't even walk straight, looking like she been hitting the bottle."

The other adults would laugh too, slapping their knees, shaking their heads. "That baby do look drunk! Look at her trying to stand up—she finna fall right over!"

I didn't know what liquor was. Didn't know why that was funny. I just knew people laughed when they said my name—and not the good kind of laugh. The kind that made me feel small. The kind that made me wonder if I was the punchline.

The second story: That one came from Uncle Milton—bless his soul.

He said it was because of the way I scooted across the floor. Diapered butt in the air, knees sliding like wheels. "Scoochy-hoochy," he'd laugh, watching me motor across Grandma's kitchen floor, chasing after Nickie or trying to get to wherever the grown-ups were.

"Look at that baby scoochy-hoochy across that floor! She's going somewhere!" He'd clap, delighted by my determination.

And just like that, the name stuck.

Scoochy-hoochy became Hoochy. The "scoochy" part fell away like baby teeth, leaving just Hoochy behind— harder, sharper, more lasting.

Sleeping @ 662

AGE 5 — NIGHTMARES, BED-WETTING, AND THE HOUSE THAT HELD MY HURT

At the top of the stairs, the first room on the right held bunk beds. Sheritta took the bottom bunk, and Nickie and I shared the top. It felt familiar—but it wasn't home. The room smelled different from 657. Not bad, just... not ours. Grandma's house carried the scent of Ben-Gay and Vicks VapoRub, of mothballs tucked in closet corners, of Pine-Sol mopped across every surface until it gleamed. At Momma's house, it smelled like cigarettes, I think, and whatever was cooking—or not. A lived-in internal chaos.

The bunk bed frame was metal, painted white, chipped in places where the rust showed through like old scabs. The mattress sagged in the middle from years of other bodies—other children—who'd slept here before us. The springs creaked every time one of us moved, announcing our restlessness to the whole house. Sheritta claimed the bottom bunk without asking, spreading herself out like she owned it. She was older, so that's just how it was. Nickie and I climbed the wobbly ladder to the top, our small bodies pressed together in the narrow space.

Nickie—my built-in best friend, my partner in everything. At night, after Grandma turned off the lights and told us to go to sleep, we'd whisper across the darkness:

"You awake?"

"Yeah."

"You miss her?"

Silence. Then: "Yeah."

"Me too."

We didn't say who. We didn't have to.

Unk's room was just across the hall. Fat-al slept there that night. I could hear them through the thin walls, the muffled sounds of boys being boys, whispering and laughing about something we weren't allowed to know. Fat-al's voice, higher than Unk's, asked questions. Unk's deeper voice answered, patient in a way he never was with us girls. I wanted to be in there with them. With my brother. Where I felt safe.

My eyes stayed wide open, fighting exhaustion and fear of the dark. I kept looking toward the doorway, silently praying to God. *Why are we at Grandma's? When can we go home? Why is Auntie sitting outside the room like a guard?*

She was really out there—one of my aunties, planted in a chair right outside our bedroom door like a prison guard. Or a protector. I couldn't tell which. Her shadow stretched across the hallway floor, lit by the light from downstairs. Every so often I'd hear her shift in her seat, the chair legs scrape the wood, then a long, heavy sigh— as if she were carrying something too big for her body.

Why was she there? Was she keeping us in? Or keeping something out?

The questions circled my mind like vultures, picking at the edges of an understanding I couldn't quite reach. My young brain worked overtime, trying to make sense of a world that had shifted so suddenly, so completely.

The house settled around us—floorboards creaking, pipes groaning, the refrigerator humming its one-note song downstairs. Outside, the Brewsters were alive with their nighttime symphony: distant sirens, car doors slamming, someone's radio playing too loud, a man and a woman arguing three buildings over, their voices rising and falling like a sad melody.

But inside Grandma's house, everything felt muted. Muffled. Like we were underwater.

Exhaustion won. My eyes closed.

Then—"Stop! Stop!" The words tore out of me.

I jerked awake, arms swinging, and smacked Nickie. "Hoochy, what did you do that for?" Nickie's voice was thick with sleep and confusion, her small body recoiling from my flailing limbs.

The unfamiliar white sheet beneath me brought me back. I blinked, trying to wake up, trying to remember where I was. The room was dark except for the thin strip of light from the hallway.

Then it hit me—what I'd dreamed wasn't just a dream. It really happened.

The ambulance.

The white sheet.

Momma's empty eyes.

The mud still caked under my fingernails.

657 Eliot getting smaller and smaller as someone carried me away.

It wasn't a nightmare I could wake up from. It was real. It was now. It was forever.

Then I heard a faint whining—*Fat-al?*

The sound was soft, almost imperceptible, but I knew it was him. My brother cried differently than other boys—never loud, never demanding attention. He cried like he was apologizing for taking up space, for needing comfort, for being sad when everyone else was trying to hold it together.

I wanted to go to his room. My brother knew how to make me feel safe, especially when I was scared.

Fat-al was my protector in ways the adults weren't. He'd share his food when I was hungry. He'd let me tag along when other kids said I was too little. He'd hold my hand crossing the street. He never made fun of me when I couldn't find my words.

And when I was scared, the words stayed trapped inside—but the pee didn't.

"Hoochy peed in the bed again!" Nickie shouted, sliding off the wet spot, disgust written all over her face. The warmth had already turned cold against my skin. The shame burned hot in my chest. I wanted to disappear into the mattress, to sink through the metal frame.

Unk and Fat-al passed the doorway that morning, caught the smell, and laughed, calling me "pissy missy."

"Aye, Hoochy done pissed the bed again!" Unk's voice rang out, loud enough for the whole house to hear.

"Pissy missy! Pissy missy!" They sang it like a playground chant, their voices rising in cruel harmony.

Fat-al joined in, but his laughter sounded forced, uneasy—like he knew he should defend me but didn't know how without making himself a target too.

A deep anger rushed up from the same place the words were supposed to come from in me. I didn't yell—I just grunted. The sound came from somewhere primal, somewhere animal. A growl without language. Rage without articulation. It was all I had.

Sheritta grabbed me, fingernails dug into my arms, squeezing my chest inward. Her eyes met mine. "Hoochy Stop," she said, with a final shake. "Use your words." She said.

I couldn't.

Nothing would come out—I'd swallowed the pain so deep my voice refused to come out.

My tongue felt thick and useless in my mouth. The words were there—I could feel them stacking up behind my teeth like a traffic jam—but they wouldn't come out. They stayed trapped, rotting inside me, turning into something darker than language.

So I swallowed them. Again and again. Until swallowing became my default. Until silence became my native tongue.

Bed-wetting is a language spoken by traumatized children—a body's way of crying when the mouth won't open, when the words won't come, when shame is the only thing louder than need.

They called me pissy-missy, but what they didn't understand was that my body was screaming what my voice couldn't say:

I'm scared. I'm alone.

My mother is gone, and nobody is explaining where she went or if she's coming back.

The Dead Don't Need a Hospital

Over the next few days, folks drifted in and out of Grandma's house. Meanwhile, I kept trying to figure out how to get across the street to Momma's house.

The parade felt endless. Each day brought new faces and voices, new dishes wrapped in aluminum foil: fried chicken, macaroni and cheese, potato salad, greens, sweet potato pie, pound cake. Food crowded every surface in Grandma's kitchen—on the stove, the counters, the ivory table, even the top of the refrigerator.

"Mmm-hmm, Pearl, I brought you some of that chicken you like," one woman would say, her voice all syrup and sympathy that didn't quite reach her eyes.

"Chile, I know you got a house full, so I made extra," another would add, setting down yet another casserole dish.

They'd hug Pearl, pat her shoulder, whisper the things I wasn't supposed to hear: "Such a shame... so young... those poor babies... drugs are the devil... she never had a chance..."

Then they'd look at us—me, Nickie, Sheritta, Fat-al— with a mix of pity and curiosity that made my skin crawl, as if they were trying to see the damage, to measure how broken we were, to guess which of us would end up like Shanky.

One afternoon, while I sat on the porch staring across the street toward home, a woman stopped by.

I'd been plotting how to get across that wide street—it seemed impossibly vast, like an ocean I couldn't swim. Cars rushed past, engines roaring like angry beasts, and I was so small. My legs were short; I knew I couldn't run fast enough if one came speeding toward me.

Eliot Street had never seemed so wide before. When Momma was alive, crossing it was nothing—a few quick steps, looking both ways like she taught me—and I'd be at Grandma's door. Now the distance had multiplied. The street had become a chasm I couldn't bridge.

657 Eliot sat there, watching me watch it. Its windows were dark. No curtains moved. No screen door opened. No Momma appeared to wave me home.

The woman who approached had kind eyes that crinkled when she smiled. Her floral dress swayed as she climbed the porch steps, a covered dish in her hands— probably more potato salad or pie, like all the others bringing food and hushed words I didn't fully understand.

Her shoes clicked against the concrete—black church shoes with a small heel, scuffed at the toes from years of wear. A run laced up the back of her left stocking, but she either didn't notice or didn't care. Her hair was pressed and curled, pinned back with bobby pins that caught the sunlight.

"Hello there, sweetheart," the woman said, settling herself down on the porch step beside me.

She didn't ask permission; she just sat, like she belonged there, like she knew I needed company even though I hadn't asked for it.

The step groaned under her weight. She smoothed her dress over her knees, set the dish beside her, then turned to look at me with those kind, crinkled eyes.

I didn't answer. I kept my eyes on Momma's house across the street, studying the door for any sign of movement, any shadow that might be her. The curtains had been drawn for days. The house looked empty. Abandoned. Dead.

"You're watching for your momma, aren't you?" the woman asked gently.

Her voice had that church-woman sound—soft but strong, like she'd spent years singing hymns and praying over other people's pain.

I nodded, not trusting my voice. My throat felt tight, the way it did when I was trying not to cry.

"Hey, dear," she said. "I'm sorry to hear 'bout your sick mother."

Sick mother? I asked with my eyes, full of questions, but made no sound.

She reached over and patted my knee, her hand warm and dry. "She's in a better place," she said softly, leaning in like she was whispering a secret. "The Lord—He's a doctor in the sickroom, a healer in the hospital, and..."

The front door pushed open, cutting her whisper short. Grandma's voice called out: "Sister Madeline, that you out there? Come on in here and get out this heat."

The woman—Sister Madeline—smiled at me one more time, squeezed my knee, and stood, brushing her dress. "You remember what I said, baby. The Lord got her now."

And I knew then—Momma was in the hospital. She was sick again, like that time when my sister found her throwing up and barely able to walk. She had left for a few days, they said, to get well.

The pieces clicked—sick equals hospital. The hospital equals getting better. Get better equals come home.

The logic was simple. Perfect. But Wrong.

"Can I tell you a secret?" Sister Madeline asked, pausing before she went inside. I turned to look at her, curious despite the ache in my chest.

She knelt down, her knees cracking, bringing herself to my eye level. Up close, I could see the powder caked in the lines around her mouth, the small mole on her chin, the way her lipstick had bled into the tiny wrinkles around her lips.

"When I was 'bout your age, maybe a lil' older, I had to stay with my auntie for a while. My momma was sick, and she needed time to get better. I ain't understand it then—I thought she ain't want me no more, that I'd done something to make her send me away. I used to sit on my auntie's porch, just like you doing now, and stare at the road that led back to my house, wishing I could walk down it and go home."

"Did you?" My voice cracked, and I had to stop and swallow hard. "Did you ever go home?"

She smiled, and this time it reached her eyes, pushing away some of the sadness. "I did. It took a while—longer than I wanted—but eventually my mama got better, and I went home."

The lie was kind. Merciful. Adults did that—told you what you needed instead of what was true. I didn't know then that her mama probably hadn't gotten better. That "going home" might have meant something different than I imagined. Sometimes, people told stories to children not because they were true, but because they were necessary.

She lifted the dish. "I should get this food inside to your grandma before it gets warm. But I want you to remember something, okay? God is with you and loves you." She went inside, leaving me alone on the porch again.

I sat there a long time after she left, watching the cars go by, counting them like sheep. One, two, three, four. Each one that passed was another barrier between me and home, another reason I couldn't cross.

A blue Cadillac with a dented fender. A rusted-out Chevy Nova blasting Marvin Gaye. A yellow taxi with a passenger in the back. A delivery truck rattling over potholes. A burgundy Buick moving slow, the driver's arm hanging out the window.

Still, I kept watching, hoping that maybe tomorrow, or the day after, or the day after that, the ambulance would bring Momma back home. She would appear on her porch and wave me over. And when she did, I'd find a way across that street, no matter how wide it seemed, no matter how fast the cars were going.

I'd find a way home.

Headed to the Hospital?

"Let's go!" Grandma yelled upstairs for all of us to come down. "We're finna go see your momma!"

At the hospital? I asked in my head.

My heart leaped. Sister Madeline's words—doctor in the sickroom, healer in the hospital—rushed back. Momma was getting better. She was ready to see us. Maybe she'd come home today. Maybe everything would go back to normal.

I skipped every other step, too excited to walk. The pounding feet of five kids thundered down the stairs toward the front door.

We were a stampede of hope, of need, of children who just wanted their mother back. Our feet hit the stairs in chaotic rhythm—boom-boom-boom-boom—like drums announcing something important.

Through the bottom of the screen door, we could see a long black car waiting outside.

I pressed my fingers to the screen, leaving little prints as I pointed. "Look! Look at that car!" I said.

It was so shiny, so long, with rows of windows. The chrome gleamed in the sunlight like jewelry. The paint was so black it looked wet. And when the door opened, there were so many seats—more than I'd ever seen in a car.

"That's a limousine," Unk said, his voice filled with awe. "A lemon-zeen?" I repeated, getting the word wrong.

"Limousine, stupid," Sheritta corrected, but even she sounded impressed.

Fat-al pressed his nose to the glass, breath fogging the window, his voice muffled when he spoke. "Why we getting picked up in a limousine? Momma must be real important now."

The way he said it made my chest tighten.
 I wanted to believe him— that the shiny car meant good news, that important people only rode in limousines when something happy had happened.
 But deep down, I knew better.
 I could feel when something wasn't right.

Grandma sat in front, and the rest of us swarmed the back, laughing and bouncing, touching all the buttons— making the windows roll up and down, lights flickering above our heads.

"Stop touching everything!" Sheritta snapped, but she was touching things too—running her fingers over the smooth leather seats, opening and closing the little compartments, marveling at the carpet on the floor.

Nickie and I sat pressed together, our small bodies swallowed by the huge seat. Everything smelled like leather and air freshener—fake pine trying to cover up the grief soaked into the upholstery from all the other families this car had carried before.

"Grandma, we going to the hospital?" I asked, my voice small and hopeful.

Grandma didn't turn around. Her shoulders were stiff, her back rigid. "Yeah, baby. We going to see your momma."

The ride felt exciting—hopeful.

Detroit passed by the windows like a movie. We drove down streets I recognized—past the corner store where Momma used to send me for cigarettes, past the playground where the older kids hung out, past Shiloh Baptist Church with its white steeple reaching toward heaven.

The city was alive with Saturday afternoon energy. People walked in little clusters, talking and laughing. Music poured from open windows. Kids played in fire hydrant spray, their bodies glistening and joyful. Old men sat on stoops playing checkers. Women hung laundry on lines strung between buildings.

Everything looked normal. The world kept spinning like nothing had changed.

How could that be? How could the sun still shine and the music still play and people still laugh when Momma was gone?

But she wasn't gone, I reminded myself. She was in the hospital. Getting better. Coming home soon.

When we arrived, the building looked like a hospital. Sort of. I stared up at the massive doors that slid open when someone stood in front of them. The building was made of red brick, like the Brewsters', but cleaner. Newer. The windows had thick curtains pulled across them. The sign out front had words I couldn't read, but there was a symbol—hands pressed together in prayer.

The automatic doors whooshed open, and I bolted through them like I was running bases, afraid they'd close and trap me outside or cut me in half like a magic trick gone wrong.

The air changed. It smelled like old people and mints.

Not hospital smell—no antiseptic, no bleach, no smell of sickness barely contained. This was different. Perfume and old lady soap. Peppermints and mothballs. Flowers—so many flowers the scent was almost choking. And underneath it all, something else. Something I didn't have a name for yet.

Death. It smelled like death.

The last hospital I remembered had beeping and voices over speakers. This place was different.

Too quiet. Too still. No nurses rushing around. No gurneys being wheeled down hallways. No overhead pages calling doctors to different rooms.

Just silence. And organ music playing softly from somewhere I couldn't see—sad, churchy music that made my stomach hurt.

In each room, a person lay inside, and the doors weren't numbered. Instead, they had letters—A, B, C—with "Parlor" written before them.

"Grandma, what's a polar?" I asked, squinting up at the sign. She didn't slow down. "Parlor, Hoochy. Not polar. It's where people say goodbye."

"Like the North Pole?" I whispered, still confused.

"No, baby. Just... it's a room."

Her voice was tight. Controlled. Like she was holding back something too big to let out here, in this place, in front of all these people.

We passed the first room. Then the second. People I didn't know, lying still in boxes lined with white silk.

Caskets. They were caskets. But I didn't know that word yet.

My feet moved, but my mind stayed behind, trying to understand. Why were there beds with lids? Why were people sleeping with their hands folded like they were praying? Why was everyone dressed so nicely—suits and dresses and jewelry—like they were going to church but lying down instead of sitting up? Each step closer, my heart beat faster. Each door we passed, I wondered—Is she in this one?

The people in the boxes looked fake. Like wax figures. Like dolls someone had arranged carefully and then forgotten.

An old woman with silver hair and rouge on her cheeks. A young man in a military uniform, his face smooth and unlined. A teenage girl in a pink dress, her hands holding a single white rose.

I tugged Grandma's hand. "Is Momma in the polar?"

"She's in Parlor C," Grandma said quietly, her voice tight and short.

I was desperate to see Momma. My hand loosened from Grandma's grip, holding on by just one finger now. My body pulled forward, my hand slipping back.

Finally, we arrived at Parlor C.

I still called it Polar in my head.

The walkway in Parlor C was lined with burgundy chairs, like the place Grandma sat for hours the other day—the welfare office.

The same kind of chairs—metal frames with thin padding, designed for waiting. For enduring. Not for comfort.

No nurses in white this time—just a preacher. Just flowers and sad faces. So many flowers. Arrangements on stands, bouquets on tables, wreaths propped on easels. Lilies and roses and carnations and flowers I didn't have names for. The smell was overwhelming—sweet and cloying, trying to cover up something underneath.

The dark rooms. The still bodies. The endless flowers. The lights over the beds. Chairs lined up for visitors. Sad music echoing through sterile halls.

Please let it be a hospital, I prayed silently. And the bed my mom was lying in, up front in the room labeled Polar C—let it be temporary. Let her get up and come home.

For a moment, I thought—Maybe this was a special kind of hospital. A fancy one where rich people went. Maybe the flowers meant she was important. Maybe the preacher was there to pray her back to health.

We sat in the front row facing Momma's bed, my siblings and me in church clothes. Then I climbed off the burgundy metal folding chair.

The clothes were stiff and uncomfortable. Someone had dressed us this morning—I couldn't remember who. The dress I wore was too big, probably Sheritta's hand-me-down, with lace at the collar that scratched my neck. My shoes pinched my toes. My socks kept sliding down into my heels.

Fat-al wore a suit that made him look like a miniature old man. Unk kept pulling at his tie like it was choking him. Nickie sat perfectly still, her hands folded in her lap, her face blank. Sheritta stared straight ahead, her jaw clenched—one large tear falling at a time, as if her eyes had a leak.

I went looking for my grandmother.

I pushed past bodies, bouquets, and stiff, awkward silence. My heart pounded, but I moved with the boldness only a child desperate for comfort can summon.

People stepped aside as I passed—not because they saw me, but because they didn't want a kid underfoot. Their conversations stopped and started around me like I was a rock in a stream:

"...so young..."

"...left four children..."

"...drugs, you know..."

"...shame what it do to families..."

Everywhere I looked, familiar faces blurred together—neighbors, church folks, relatives I'd seen once or twice at Thanksgiving—then one face pulled me forward.

I extended my neck, straining between the bodies to see him.

He was tall—too tall for the room. Slim, with thick glasses that hid more than they revealed. We called them coke-bottle glasses because of how thick they were. His Afro slanted forward, neat but weary.

A knot swelled in his throat, like he'd swallowed a stone that refused to move.

His legs rose like the lampposts on Eliot. His arms were long, like they'd been created from tree branches. His hands were larger than my brother's baseball mitt, and they looked ruined—skin mottled with bruises and scars, pocked with black pits like burns. The swelling left his fingers stiff, too puffy to close into a fist.

Track marks. Years of them. Some old and faded, some fresh and angry. His veins had collapsed, leaving lumpy ridges under the skin.

And then his face—tired in a way sleep could never heal. Skin sagged in some places, pulled tight in others. Waxy. Pale where there should've been warmth. The color had drained out, leaving patches that mapped grief and something nameless.

His cheeks hollowed, bones sharp against thinning skin. His eyes—red-rimmed and cloudy—wandered when not forced to hold still. He twitched, scratched, wiped at sweat that kept returning.

He looked sick. As sick as Momma had been. As sick as the people in the other parlors.

"Hoochy..." he said, his voice deep and rough but soft enough to pull me closer. "Hey, baby girl, it's me. Your dad."

I froze. The word dad didn't fit the air. It sounded like something I should know but didn't—like a song half-remembered from a dream.

Back then, I didn't have the language for what I felt. I only knew the heaviness in my chest, the way my stomach twisted like it was trying to hide. I knew faces, not fathers. Voices, not promises. And his voice—low, tired, smelling faintly of cigarettes and something sharp—felt both familiar and foreign.

Now, thinking back, I know what I couldn't name that day:
What do you call a father who's more ghost than man?
Who shows up at funerals but not birthdays?
Who knows your nickname but not your address?
Who carries the same darkness in his veins that your mother's veins once told you?

Daddy?

The dead don't need hospitals. But the living need answers.

Anger Watching Over Me

"Grandma!" I screamed, more breath than sound.

I searched the crowd again and again for her but saw only other faces marked by the same sickness, the same restless shadow—like the tall man who claimed to be my father.

Addicts. The room was full of them. I didn't know the word then, but I knew the look—that hollowed-out quality, that twitchiness, that way of being physically present but somehow gone.

Momma's friends. Momma's acquaintances. Momma's running partners. People who'd been at 657 Eliot at all hours, coming and going, whispering in corners, disappearing into the bathroom together.

They were all here now, dressed in their best clothes, trying to look respectable. Trying to look like they hadn't had a hand in this. Trying to look like mourners instead of accomplices.

"If no one is going to take all of them, then no one is taking any of them."

It was Grandmother. Her tone was sharp enough to slice through bone.

The voice cut through the organ music, the hushed conversations, and the pounding of my own heartbeat in my ears.

I followed it to a small room crowded with adults.

A side room off the main parlor—probably meant for the family to gather, to steal private moments away from the viewing. But this wasn't a tender family gathering. This was a negotiation. Division. The distribution of goods, except the goods were us. Were children. Were me.

One auntie was there—the one who stayed with us that night. The one I adored. Beautiful, bright, and with one child, her son, whom I loved like a brother. He was my best friend whenever we saw each other on holidays or days like this.

She wore a black dress that hugged her curves, her hair pressed and curled, her makeup perfect despite the tears that had tracked through it earlier. She looked like someone who had her life together. Someone who could take on more responsibility if she wanted to.

Another auntie stood nearby—the one who scared me. She rarely smiled. Her face looked ill, like my mother's did in her final days.

Sunken cheeks. Yellow-tinged eyes. Skin that looked paper-thin and bruised too easily. She'd been pretty once—you could still see it in the bone structure, but something had stolen that beauty and left this hollow shell behind.

She crossed her arms tight over her chest, a wall. She didn't want this conversation. None of them did.

I don't remember who else was in that room.

Just voices. Male and female. Young and old. Family and friends and people who felt obligated to show up and offer opinions on what should be done with Shanky's kids.

"No! We're not splitting them up!" Grandmother barked. Her voice was iron. Final. The voice she used when someone tested her—and lost.

What came next—I still don't know if I truly heard it or if someone told me later.

Maybe both.

Maybe I heard it that day and blocked it out, and years later someone confirmed what my memory had tried to protect me from. Or maybe I didn't hear it at all—maybe I was too far away, too small to understand—and the story got told and retold until it became my memory even though it wasn't mine.

Either way, I know what was said.

One auntie said, "I can take the older girl to help me with my son while I go to work and school."

Translation: I need a babysitter, and Sheritta's old enough to be useful.

The other said, "I'll take the boy. I already have two sons. One more won't make no difference."

Translation: Boys are easier. Boys don't ask questions. Boys don't need as much attention.

But Nickie and Hoochy?

"They're too young," she said. "They can still go into foster care. Maybe get adopted. Young enough somebody might want'em. Young enough they might forget all this."

Translation: They're deadweight. Baggage. Too little to be useful, too damaged to be wanted.

As they looked at each other, I pushed the door open a little wider to get a better look at my grandmother's face. It could be hard to read sometimes—she didn't have any eyebrows, but those lips told it all.

Grandma had drawn her eyebrows on that morning with a brown pencil, two thin arches that gave her a look of perpetual surprise or suspicion, depending on her mood. But right now, with her face screwed up in disgust, those drawn-on eyebrows couldn't convey what her mouth did.

Her lips poked so far out you would think she'd sucked on a sour lemon.

Her bottom lip jutted forward, her jaw set, her nostrils flaring. This was Grandma at her most formidable, unmovable, unshakable, absolutely done with the bullsh!!

"NO!" She placed her hands on her hips, fists clenched.

The word exploded out of her like a shotgun blast, silencing every other voice in that cramped room.

She turned to leave, took one step, then spun back when a hand grabbed her shoulder.

"Pearl, now wait—"

"Naw, don't 'Pearl' me—"

"We're just trying to figure out what's best—"

"Best? Best for who? Y'all talking 'bout splitting up these babies like they furniture you dividing up!"

"We ain't got the resources—"

"I ain't got the resources neither! You think I got money just laying around? You think I'm young enough to be raising babies again? I'm tired! I done raised my kids, and look how that turned out!"

Her voice cracked on that last part. The façade broke just for a second, revealing the grief underneath—grief for Shanky, grief for all the ways she'd failed or felt she'd failed, grief for having to do this all over again when she should've been resting, should've been done.

"What do you want us to do?" they asked Grandmother.

The question hung in the air, heavy and hopeless. And I burst into the room, heart first. In my imagination, at least.

In my imagination, I screamed, "I hate you all!" In my imagination, I told them exactly what I thought—how dare they talk about us like we weren't people, like we didn't have feelings, like we couldn't hear them deciding our fates like judges at a slave auction.

In my imagination, I was brave. Fierce. The Hoochy everyone thought I was.

All of them turned to me and said, "We're sorry, Hoochy, we love you," as they smothered me with hugs and kisses.

Nope. That didn't happen.

Remember what I said at the beginning about the things you're told, the things you believe, the stories that turn into memories? Have you ever seen a movie where the actor imagines himself being brave and rescuing someone, then snaps back to the same spot, wishing it was true?

Well, that was this moment. My mouth stayed closed. Like always.

I stood in that doorway, small and silent and invisible, watching the adults decide my future without asking what I wanted, without asking if I had an opinion, without acknowledging that I was a human being with thoughts and feelings and preferences.

Where was this bold, feared, fierce "Hoochy" now?

Nowhere. She didn't exist yet. She was still being formed, still gathering evidence, still collecting reasons to build walls so high nobody could ever hurt her again.

And for a long time, I didn't speak. Not really. Not because I couldn't. But because no one seemed to be listening. Not to me.

That was me. Even then, I knew how to vanish in a room full of people. But deep down, I wanted to be seen. Not just called. Seen.

And somehow, through all of that, a piece of me kept hoping. Hoping someone will notice. Wanting to matter. And maybe, one day, I'd be more than a nickname and a name on someone's list. Someone's burden. Maybe I'd be known.

I began to be known, alright—but known for being ugly, poor, a burden to others.

The first time I remember feeling that way was at my mother's funeral.

Actually, it was before that. It was always. But the funeral made it official. Made it public. Made it permanent.

What made me different... was my name. My nickname.

That name followed me like a second skin. Not just because people called me that—but because somewhere along the way, it became who I was. It stuck. It settled deep into my skin before I even had the words to push it away.

When would she speak? When would she show them?

As I crawled under the table where folks gathered and talked, I balled up with my knees to my chest.

The table was in the corner of the side room, covered with a white cloth that hung down almost to the floor. It made a perfect hiding place cave where I could disappear while still hearing everything.

My dress bunched up around my thighs. My shoes pressed against my bottom. I wrapped my arms around my shins and made myself as small as possible.

That's when it came. Not in a face, not in a hand reaching for me, but in a voice that rose inside my chest. Heavy, firm, older than me.

Anger: They don't want you. Do you hear them? Every single excuse is another way of saying not you.

Me : But... I need somebody.

Anger: No. You don't. You don't need anyone. Not them. Not your momma, not God. You've got me.

Me: But I'm little.

Anger: Then I'll make you big. I'll stand in front when no one else will. I'll keep you from crying in front of them. I'll shut the door so they can't get in. You don't need anybody else. You don't even need love. You need strength.

Me: But it hurts.

Anger: Let me carry it. Just close the door on love. Shut it down. If you let me in, continue to trust me, no one will ever leave you again. Not really. Because I'll always be here.

Like the scripture says, let me carry your burden. The verse sounded familiar, like what I heard in Sunday School.

Except it wasn't God speaking. It was Anger. And Anger sounded a lot like God to a five-year-old girl who'd been abandoned by everyone who was supposed to love her.

And so, I listened. I shut the door. And Anger stayed.

Not from the room. Not from Him. From myself. From feeling. From needing. From hoping.

I shut the door on the little girl who wanted to be held, who wanted to matter, who wanted someone to fight for her the way Grandma was fighting for all of us.

And I let Anger move in. Made it comfortable. Gave it a permanent place at the table.

"Mrs. Carr, we're ready to proceed to the graveyard," the man said, dressed in a black suit so clean and stiff he could barely lift his arms as he reached for my grandmother.

The funeral director. Somber and professional, with a voice like warm honey, designed to soothe the grieving. Her resentment didn't disappear, but her commitment to keeping us together was stronger.

Grandma had made her decision. She'd drawn her line in the sand. We were hers, now—all of us, whether she was ready or not, whether she had the resources or not, whether she had the energy or not.

She came out of the room, yelling, "Hoochy, come on here, girl. We got to go." That name again. Loud and lasting.

It didn't feel pretty. Or soft. But it felt strong.

And maybe that's what God knew I'd need—something strong enough to hold me when the world let go because that name was all I had when I buried my momma. When I met my daddy. When I learned that even love can leave you behind.

The rest of that day is gone—blank. I don't remember the graveyard, the prayers, or the dirt. Trauma does that. Erases what's too painful to keep. Leaves holes where memories should be.

I don't remember if I cried. I don't remember if they lowered the casket while we watched or if they did it after we left. I don't remember if anyone held my hand or if I stood alone.

I don't remember saying goodbye. But I do remember what came next. A few days later, we went back to the real hospital.

Not for Momma. For me.

The bed-wetting hadn't stopped. Neither had nightmares. Neither had the silence that had swallowed my voice whole.

It was grief. It was trauma. My body was trying to hold a kind of hurt it didn't understand. The doctors ran tests. Checked my bladder. I didn't know how to answer the questions I was asked.

"Does it hurt when you pee?"

Sometimes. Not really. I don't know.

"Do you feel it happening?"

No—Not until it's too late.

"Are you scared of something?"

Everything. Nothing. I don't know.

They said nothing was wrong. Physically, I was fine. But even at five, I could feel something wasn't fine—something inside me didn't work right.

Later, I'd hear the whispers.

Somebody said maybe Momma had taken something while she was pregnant with me. That she was "using." Maybe I came out with problems because of it. They said it quietly, like secrets that only grown folks could say out loud. I didn't understand what they meant, but I felt it—how the room got heavy when my name came up.

How eyes would glance away like I wasn't supposed to hear. Like I was something broken before I ever had a chance to be whole.

"It's psychological," the doctor told Grandma. "She's been through a trauma. This is her body's response. She'll grow out of it. Just be patient."

Patient. As if patience was something Grandma had in abundance. As if patience would stop the smell of urine from soaking into mattresses, would stop the teasing from my siblings, would stop the shame from eating me alive.

"Ain't nothing wrong with her but stubbornness," Grandma muttered on the drive home. "She can hold it if she wants to. She just don't want to."

But she was wrong.

I couldn't hold it. I couldn't hold anything—not my pee, not my tears, not my voice, not my hope. Everything leaked out of me in ways I couldn't control.

And all I could do was ball up under tables, shut doors inside myself, and let Anger tell me what to do. But deep down, I wanted my momma to pull me out of that darkness, to tell Anger to leave me alone. But she wasn't there. And Anger knew it, and whispered that I didn't need her anyway—that Shanky didn't want to be Momma, not to me. Anger said I didn't need Jesus or anyone. Only silence.

Even though I did.
Even though I desperately, achingly, impossibly did.

Shanky's Shadow
THE SHADOW OF A WOMAN I FEARED BECOMING

My earliest memory of speaking—really using my voice—was the day she put me in Jackson.

Yes, Jackson. Not prison. The punishment.

Let me explain.

Your face to the wall. Arms stretched high, fingers splayed and pressed flat. Legs pushed back until your heels floated; all weight balanced on tiptoes. Spine locked, stiff as rebar. Neck bent forward, forehead grazing the wall but not touching.

You held it. Didn't slip. Didn't sag. If you did, start over. Five more minutes.

My mother had strict rules for the four of us: Sheritta, the oldest. Gerald (Fat-al), the only boy. Nicole (Nickie). And my name? Yolanda, by birth.

Only used for kindergarten roll call and Sunday School attendance.

Everywhere else—home, street, church porch—I was Hoochy. One morning, I woke on the thin mattress I shared with Nickie. No frame. No box spring. Just padding on cold cement.

I slid off, bare feet silent, and crept to the door.

The hallway was tight and dark. Paint peeling in curls like dead skin. I smelled it first—something frying. Heard the grease pop and sizzle.

Momma was up. Cooking. I peeked out, just my head past the door frame. Shanky didn't play. When she said stay in the room, she meant it.

Break the rule? Jackson.

Arms burning. Toes trembling. Back locked in place— the shake in your calves, the ache in your fingers numb from pressing, your shoulders screaming as time dragged.

Five years old and already feeling like Stretch Armstrong. You'd have to know my generation's toys to get it.

People say mothers don't have favorites. That's a lie.

Shanky had favorites. We all knew it.

The oldest and Nickie, her girls. She'd sit Nickie on her lap during TV shows, kiss her cheeks, stroke her hair like it was gold. I don't remember being kissed like that. Don't remember being pulled in close.

I have one memory of a hug—maybe. It feels soft and blurred, like a dream I might've made up just so I could say I had one.

Shanky loved us. But she loved men more. And drugs more than that. That's just the truth.

Still, our house looked like a home. Floors clean. Kitchen stocked. Furniture matching. No screaming, no broken things, no mess you could point to and say, That's why it hurt.

But the rules whispered what the silence wouldn't say.

Stay out of her room. Don't come out until she calls.

Go outside when company comes. I didn't understand. I was young, but not stupid. I didn't get why we had to vanish just to make space for her life. Why being near her meant being invisible.

That's why I rebelled.

That's why I broke the rules.

They folded. I didn't.

So I was the problem child. The hard-headed one. Still am. I was born with complications. The hospital said a disability, as if that was the whole story. Like I was stamped with it. Like that was all I'd ever be. But that wasn't my fault. That's what happens when a baby grows inside a body used like an ashtray. Pills, powder, men—everything but love.

I carried the damage, but I didn't cause it.

And still... it became mine to own. My burden. My proof. My fight.

Sometimes I wonder if she ever wanted me at all. If she looked at me and saw what they said—a mistake. A regret.

I wasn't what she planned. Just what happened.

But I needed to be more than that. I need to believe I was born on purpose. That my life wasn't just an afterthought from someone else's broken moment.

They called her T-Shanky. "T" for Tough.

But to the neighborhood? She was just another dope fiend.

That dope fiend on Eliot with all those kids.

I heard it whispered on porches.

She was tiny—four-foot-eleven—but nothing about her felt small. A real-life Black Betty Boop: curves sharp enough to hurt, voice sweet enough to lie.

She pulled people in—especially men. A beauty that became currency, then a trap. And that's part of what ruined her. Or maybe what saved her, in whatever form survival took back then.

I don't remember much about her. And I won't smear her name. I just want to show you the version of her I knew—or maybe the one I never got to know.

We learned early that we only had each other, Sheritta, Gerald, and Nickie.

Why?

Because Shanky had her own life, she loved us—in her own way—but not equally. Not out loud. Not the kind of love you could lean on when your knees gave out. Maybe it was who our fathers were. Maybe how we looked.

Or maybe... maybe because her life got stolen before she could figure out how to live it.

Pregnant at fifteen. Four kids by twenty. She never got to be a child, never got to be held without expectation. So how could she offer that to us?

She had demons. Real ones. They sat with her, slept beside her. Whispered that she wasn't enough, that the pain was permanent.

By five, I already knew: my mother wouldn't love us more than the life that killed her.

I remember once reaching for her hand. Big hands, too big for such a small woman, but I didn't care. I just wanted to feel her grip mine.

Two minutes later, a knock hit the door.

"Go to your room," she said, eyes already gone.

And that was it. The end. Of her, for the rest of that day.

That kind of rejection? It doesn't shout. It sits in your chest, quiet and solid like a locked box.

One afternoon, her door was left open. Of course, I looked. Of course, I snuck. That's what Hoochy did.

She was laid out across her bed—a real bed, not a mattress on the floor like the one Nickie and I shared.

This one had a box spring. A headboard. Clean covers. Her arms dangled off the side, limp, and a plastic band cinched tight around her arm.

I didn't understand what I was seeing. What was that for? Is she alive?

"Hoochy, get back in the room," said Sheritta—Re-Re to Shanky, but never to us. She didn't get a nickname. Just responsibility.

At seven, Sheritta was already part-mother to us. Cooking. Cleaning. Waking us up. Walking herself to school. She didn't ask for it, but it became hers—we became hers. Was that why she was Shanky's favorite? Because she absorbed all the weight?

Pearl—our grandmother, Shanky's mom—had three daughters and one son. Shanky was the second born. Her siblings had their own kids, too. The only one still living at home was our Unk, quiet and strange, a ghost floating through the house when we came to stay.

Shanky was known for her voice. People said it sounded like Mahalia Jackson. I remember hearing it sometimes on good days—soft gospel floating down the hall while she cleaned. But only Nickie and I were kept in our room. Sheritta and Gerald—we called him Fat-al—helped with chores.

Fat-al got his nickname from the show Fat Albert—big eyes, full cheeks, round face, always looking like he was mid-laugh or mid-thought. He had his demons, too, but they came later.

Shanky's blood ran strong. You could see her in all of us. Sheritta had her beauty.

Nickie, too, but with an early, aching prettiness—men noticed far too soon.

That voice? They both had it.

Fat-al and I looked like our father. Maybe that's why Shanky looked at us differently. Maybe that's why she... couldn't love us out loud.

But Fat-al had her heart. Her brightness.

He didn't make it out of high school, but his mind was quick. He could answer almost every question Alex Trebek asked on Jeopardy when we watched together. He felt everything, too sensitive, they said—but he had to hide it, because if he didn't, he'd be called a punk or "Si"—short for sissy, rhyming with my nickname, "Pissy."

And me? What part of her did I get? Her fight.

That I don't take-no-stuff, steel-in-your-bones toughness, that was mine. I inherited her wall. I reinforced it with my own hands.

Early that morning, before I got the okay to come out—because another rule said that while Sheritta, Fat-al, and Nickie got ready for school, I had to stay out of the way—the front door didn't slam when they left; it eased shut with a deep, solid thud that echoed off the walls. Then came the sharp, metallic click of the lock sliding into place. The sound faded. Minutes later, the same door opened again with a soft hush as someone came in.

I began to open my bedroom door, slowly turning the handle, trying to keep Momma from hearing me. I stood between the frame and the slight gap, scared of Jackson if she caught me.

I saw her argue with a man. I don't know who he was, just that it was only me and her in the house when he came.

First, it was voices. Then shouting.

He pushed her into a chair.

She fell—but not fully. It was controlled, like she wanted to drop.

Then, as planned, she reached into the couch cushion and pulled out a knife. Not just a kitchen knife. This thing looked like something out of a movie. Curved. Long. Bright enough to make your eyes squint.

He backed away fast. "Shanky, you crazy! You're a mean b—" he shouted, backing toward the door.

She didn't flinch. Just stood, one shoe missing, clothes torn, sweat on her face like fire.

And somehow... I was standing there. I don't remember coming into that room—breaking the "don't come out the room" rule—but I was there.

She saw me. Her voice changed—sharp first, then soft. "Don't you ever let any man hurt you," she said. "You protect yourself."

But I didn't turn right away. The tone wasn't the usual punishment tone. It didn't carry that sharp, no-nonsense edge. No, this time... it carried something else.

It was the voice of a woman who had just stood face to face with a giant—not with a slingshot, but with something heavier: faith.

I could hear the tremble riding beneath her words, barely masked. I could see it in the tension in her arms, the fire in her eyes—not rage, but holy fear turned fight. I could sense the relief like smoke rising off her skin, curling in the air between us.

And I could feel her heartbeat—yes, I felt it—not just in her chest, but through the soles of her feet, traveling across the floor and up into me like a living drumbeat.

Boom. Boom. Boom.

Each beat said: You're safe now.

Each beat said: Not today.

Each beat said: God still sees me.

And I stood there—five years old, too young to name it, but old enough to recognize what I'd just witnessed.

That wasn't just a mother yelling at a man. That was a woman pulling down the heavens to cover her child. That was David staring down Goliath—not with stone and sling, but with pure, wild belief that she would not lose.

And I remember thinking: That's what love is. Not the soft kind they show on TV. Not the kind that tucks you in at night.

This love was hard. Gritted teeth. Torn clothes. One shoe on. Knife in hand. Voice shaking. But still—she stood.

That moment never left me. Even now, older, grown, and weathered, I can still hear her voice in my bones. That soft drop in her tone after the storm:

"Hoochy, get back in your room."

And the part she didn't say?

You're safe because I stood.

That was the day I watched my mother's pain turn into protection. Her sadness into strength. Her silence into a war cry.

And I carry that with me. Not just the damage—but the fight. The faith. The victory.

Because even though she couldn't always love me the way I needed, in that moment, she loved me enough to face her Goliath. And behind her trembling hands, her trembling voice, something holy holding her up.

That was God. That was grace. That was the sunshine. And I saw it. His mercy in the moments I should've been broken. His grace when I was too small to protect myself.

His arms, invisible but steady, when hers were busy with someone else. That's the light that found me—even when I wasn't looking for it.

Shanky wasn't evil. She was exhausted. She wasn't cruel on purpose.

She was just sad—and stayed sad. Because sadness that deep turns into anger. And anger raised me as much as she did.

Shanky's shadow.

Pearl's fire.

Hoochy's wall. All of it—is me.

Her Beauty in Many Ways

Shanky or T-Shanky, depending on her mode, was born Marilyn Yvonne Carr, the second of four kids my grandmother had. Not all of them shared the same father, but Benjamin Carr was "Dad" to everyone.

People noticed Shanky's beauty before she even had time to notice it herself. She wasn't out looking for men; they found her.

Tiny, with eyes the color of warm earth and lips shaped so perfectly you'd think they were drawn by hand—back then, she didn't need injections, fillers, or tattooed liner women now chase.

School never really fit her unless it involved the arts. Shanky loved to sing and dance, and though I never heard her talk much about her early years, I caught glimpses of them in childhood stories.

I remember bedtime with her the most. After giving Nickie and me a bath, she'd sit us on top of the closed toilet lid. We were so slippery with the Vaseline she rubbed into our skin; sometimes we'd slide right off, laughing, while she tried to hold us steady.

Then came prayers. She'd have us close our eyes and repeat after her:

"Matthew, Mark, Luke, and John, bless the bed I lay on, four corners to my bed, four angels overhead. God bless Momma, Daddy, Grandma... God bless everyone in the whole world."

Her voice would soften as the words tumbled out of us. Then the singing began.

She would walk backward out of the room, one hand trailing the wall until it found the light switch. She'd flick it off just as her song carried into the hallway—her voice becoming both lullaby and shield, stretching across the dark to keep us safe.

What soothed me as a child later confused me as I grew older. That same hand that turned out the light sometimes left me in the dark in other ways. That same voice that floated me to sleep could also fall silent when I needed her to speak.

I learned that a person can bring you both comfort and chaos, safety and storm.

I didn't know it then, but I was already carrying pieces of her struggle inside me. Shanky's shadow was long. And I grew up inside it.

Day After Forever

AGES 6 — WHEN FOREVER BECAME SOMETHING, I HAD TO SURVIVE

All I remember is waking up the day after the funeral at my grandmother's. I was scared of her dark rooms, the sly, mouse-eating cat, and the unfamiliar bed.

The darkness in Grandma's house was different from the darkness at 657. At Momma's, the streetlights bled through thin curtains, casting orange shadows that danced on the walls. There was always noise—music from somebody's stereo, voices rising and falling, the hum of life refusing to sleep.

But Grandma's house went silent at night. Heavy silence. The kind that pressed against your eardrums and made you hear your own heartbeat. The windows were covered with thick drapes that blocked out everything—light, sound, hope. And in that suffocating dark, every creak of the floorboards sounded like footsteps. Every settling of the old house sounded like something coming for you.

We'd stayed before, but this felt different—forced, permanent.

Before, staying at Grandma's was temporary. A sleepover. A break for Momma. "Y'all go stay with Pearl tonight—Momma got something to do." And we'd go, knowing we'd be back home in a day or two, back to our own beds, our routines, our chaos.

But this time, nobody said when we were going home. Nobody said anything at all. Her house sat across the street from Momma's. It was dark inside, smelled like old clothes, and was crowded with furniture. That cat was always eating something.

The cat was gray and mean, with eyes that glowed yellow in the dark. Grandma called him Smokey, but we called him Devil Cat when she wasn't listening. He'd hiss if you got too close, swipe at your ankles when you walked past, leave dead things at your feet on the couch. Once, at breakfast, I sat dreading my wet cornflakes and bananas while the cat devoured a mouse he'd caught from one of the many holes in the house.

The sound of it, crunch, crunch, crunch—turned my stomach. The cat sat in the corner by the radiator, proud and unbothered, bones snapping between his teeth. A tail hung from his mouth like spaghetti.

I pushed my bowl away, appetite gone. "Eat your food, Hoochy," Grandma commanded from the stove. "I ain't wasting nothing."

But I couldn't. Not with that sound. Not with the image burned into my brain. One evening, Fat-al sat on the yellow couch and rested his arm behind it. Then he screamed—something bit him.

"Ow! Something bit me! Something bit me!" Fat-al jumped up, clutching his arm, his face twisted in pain and shock. My Unk pulled the couch back—after we all shouted and jumped up—and a huge rat shot out, running toward the kitchen, disappearing beneath the sink.

It was massive. Its tail thick and scaly, dragging behind it like a snake. "Lord, have mercy!" Grandma shrieked.

"Get it! Get it!" Sheritta screamed, jumping onto a chair. Nickie started crying, holding onto me like I could protect her from anything. Unk, only a teenager but the man of the house, grabbed a broom.

He was trying to be brave, trying to step into a role he wasn't ready for—the protector, the man. His hands shook as he gripped that broom handle. "Hoochy, get your nappy head out the way!" he yelled.

The insult stung, but I ignored it. I was used to it. "Nappy head" was what they called me when my hair hadn't been combed in days, when the kitchen got too busy and nobody had time to deal with my thick, tangled mess that refused to cooperate.

I wanted to see, even though I was scared. That rat was so big it could've worn my pants. "Fat-al, here, hold the broom," Unk said. "When I open the cabinet, hit it."

Fat-al gripped the broom, his hands shaking at the top.

"Fat-al, you scared?" I asked.

"No, I'm not—shut up, ugly!" he shot back, nervously standing his ground, legs spread wide like he was ready for baseball.

Ugly. That word hit me harder than any broom ever could. It wasn't the first time I'd heard it. Wouldn't be the last, but every time, it carved a little deeper into the space where my self-worth should've been.

"I'm finna get that big stick behind the washer. I'll get him," I said, trying to skip past Fat-al.

"Hoochy, go sit down. You always trying to act like a boy." He shoved me hard, and I hit the floor.

"Grandma!" I screamed. "Fat-al hit me and punched me in the face!" I clutched my eye, Oscar-winning, crying, making that sharp hissing sound. "It hurts—my eye hurts!"

The lie came easy. Too easy. I'd learned that getting attention required exaggeration, required drama, required making myself impossible to ignore.

"Stop lying, Hoochy. I didn't hit you in the eye," Fat-al said, panic rising in his voice.

He knew what was coming. We all did.

Grandma came stomping into the kitchen. "Fat-al, get out of here!" She grabbed a coat hanger from the closet on her way in, straightening it out.

Grandma didn't play. Didn't ask questions first. Didn't wait for explanations. If someone said you did something, you were guilty until proven innocent—and even then, you were probably still guilty.

Whop. The sound of metal hitting his head, his back, his arm.

The coat hanger whistled through the air before making contact. Each hit echoed through the kitchen, punctuated by Fat-al's yelps and attempts to shield himself.

While he ducked and scrambled out, I looked back at him. When Grandma's head was turned, I removed my hand from my eye, stuck my tongue out, and mouthed, "Nah"—quick enough not to get caught.

The satisfaction was brief. Hollow. But it was something. Some small win in a life where I felt like I was losing everything.

"I hate you! I hate this house! I wish my momma was living—" Fat-al yelled as he ran.

His words hung in the air like smoke after a fire. Nobody moved. Nobody breathed.

"I do too!" my grandma yelled back.

The admission cracked something open in that kitchen. Grandma's voice broke on the last word, and for just a second, we all saw it—the grief she'd been carrying, the loss she couldn't fix, the weight of burying her daughter and inheriting her children when she was too old, too tired, too broken herself.

Me? I didn't care anymore. Anger lived in that house. So did slammed doors. Roaches and rats.

I stopped asking God why. Why this house? Why this life? Why me?

He didn't answer—not then, not ever.

Or maybe He did, and I just couldn't hear Him over the noise of survival.

Grief turns children into liars,

into snitches,

into shadows of who they might've been.

It teaches you that attention—

even angry attention—

is better than being invisible.

That winning small battles

against your siblings

feels like power

when you've lost the war

for your mother's life.

Forgive the child who lied.

Forgive the child who hurt.

Forgive the child who became

what she needed to survive.

Unk the Terrorizer

My Unk was the Dennis the Menace of 662 Eliot. He was only thirteen when we came to live with Grandma, but he ruled that house like he owned it.

Being the only boy—the man of the house—gave him power he shouldn't have had. And he used it on all of us, every chance he got.

Nickie caught it one afternoon while he was practicing his cast from the top bunk of his bed. She was just standing there when the hook snagged her right between the eyes. Blood streamed down her face while Unk stood there wide-eyed, laughing, the rod still in his hand.

"I ain't mean to!" he shouted when Grandma came running. "She got in the way!"

But Nickie hadn't moved. He just didn't care where that hook landed.

The scar stayed for years—a thin white line between her eyes; good thing she wore glasses to hide it.

Fat-al got it worse—or maybe just more humiliating. Unk would sneak into our room at night with a bowl of warm water. He'd wait until Fat-al was deep asleep, snoring soft with his mouth open, and then he'd dip my brother's hand in that water.

Every. Single. Time.

Fat-al would wake up in a wet bed, confused and ashamed, while Unk stood in the doorway laughing so hard he had to hold his stomach.

"Pissy boy! Pissy boy!" Unk would chant, slapping his hands.

And Fat-al—my protector, my big brother—would just sit there in the dark, silent, fists clenched, trying not to cry.

The humiliation cut deeper than any physical wound. Because I was the bed-wetter. That was my shame, my cross to bear. But Unk made Fat-al feel what I felt every morning—that burning embarrassment, that sense of being broken, that fear that everyone would find out.

And me? What Unk did to me—well, that mark lasted longer than any of the others.

Saturday nights were hair night. The whole routine started after dinner; first came the bath. Grandma would run the water in that old tub until it was scalding hot, then add a little cold so we wouldn't burn. We'd take turns—Sheritta first because she was the oldest, then Nickie and me. By then the water was cold and cloudy, a film of soap scum floating on top.

Then came the hair.

Grandma would sit us down in the kitchen, one by one, a towel draped over our shoulders. She'd section our hair with a comb, parting it into squares, greasing each section with Royal Crown, Blue Magic, or that tar-smelling Dax grease that came in the black jar.

That Dax smelled like a freshly paved road on a hot summer day—thick, pungent, tonic-sharp. It was supposed to help our hair grow, though I never saw proof of that. Mostly, it just made our pillows slick and our foreheads shiny.

If it was hot oil treatment night—whether we wanted it or not—Grandma would heat the tin top directly on the stove until the grease inside turned to liquid gold. Then she'd pour it onto our scalps, section by section, massaging it in with her rough, strong fingers.

"Sit still, Hoochy. This'll help your kitchen grow out."

My "kitchen", the nappy edges at the back of my neck that refused to straighten no matter how much heat or grease Grandma applied. And when that kitchen showed out, the pressing comb came out.

Grandma would set it directly on the stove burner, letting the metal teeth heat up until they glowed faintly red. You could hear it sizzling when she pulled it through our hair, sounding like bacon frying, followed by the acrid smell of burnt hair and grease.

The pressing comb was a simple tool—brass teeth, wooden handle, heavy as a weapon. It had been heating hair for generations of Black women, straightening what society said was unacceptable, taming what the world called "nappy" or "bad."

Sheritta usually did the pressing. Grandma's hands shook too much, and she'd burned us one too many times. Sheritta was steadier, more patient. She'd test the comb on a paper towel first, making sure it wasn't too hot, before running it through our hair in smooth, careful strokes.

"Hold your ear down, Hoochy. Don't move."

I'd sit perfectly still, barely breathing, terrified of that hot metal coming anywhere near my face. I'd seen the burns before—on Grandma's fingers, on Sheritta's neck, on Nickie's ear that one time she turned her head too fast.

Unk changed all that.

We were getting ready for church. Sheritta was in the kitchen pressing Nickie's hair. I was waiting my turn, sitting on the couch in my slip and socks, my hair still damp and greasy from the night before.

The pressing comb sat on the stove, heating up, its wooden handle turned out toward the room.

Unk walked into the kitchen, grabbed a spoon from the drawer, and leaned against the stove like he had all the time in the world.

"Unk, move," Sheritta said, irritation sharp in her voice. "You gon' burn yourself."

"I ain't gon' burn nothing," he shot back.

Then his eyes slid over to me.

I saw it—the shift. The idea formed behind his smirk. He reached for the pressing comb, picking it up by the handle, examining it like he'd never seen one before.

"This what y'all use?" he asked, all innocent like.

"Put it down, Unk," Sheritta warned.

But he didn't.

He turned toward me, still holding that comb, still smirking, and said, "Hoochy, hold still. Let me see something."

I should've run. I should've screamed. But I froze.

He walked over slowly, deliberately, the comb held out in front of him like a torch. And before I could move—before I could even think to move—he pressed that hot metal directly against my forehead.

The pain was instant. Blinding.

I screamed—a sound that came from somewhere deeper than my lungs.

The smell of burning skin filled the room. Thick. Nauseating. Like meat left too long on a grill.

Sheritta dropped the comb she was holding and lunged at Unk, shoving him so hard he stumbled backward into the wall.

"What is wrong with you?!" she screamed.

Grandma came running from the back room, her housecoat flapping, her face already twisted in fury.

"What happened? What happened?!"

I couldn't speak. I just sat there, hands pressed against my forehead, tears streaming down my face, the pain radiating through my skull like someone had branded me.

Unk stood there, the comb still in his hand, eyes wide like he'd surprised even himself.

"I was just playin'," he muttered. "I ain't think it was that hot."

Grandma snatched the comb from him and threw it in the sink, where it hissed against the wet metal. Then she grabbed him by the collar and dragged him toward his room.

"You don't play like that! You hear me?! You don't play like that!"

The sound of her hand hitting him echoed through the house. But I didn't feel satisfied. I didn't feel vindicated.

I just felt the burn.

Sheritta held a cold, wet rag against my forehead while Grandma finished beating Unk in the other room. The cold helped, but not much. The damage was done.

When Grandma came back, her face was tired. Worn. Like she'd used up the last bit of fight she had left.

"Let me see it," she said softly.

I moved my hand. The burn was bad—angry red, already blistering in the center. The shape of the comb teeth pressed into my skin like a brand.

Grandma went to the cabinet and pulled out a jar of Vaseline. She smeared it thick across the burn, her touch gentle for once.

"This gon' scar," she said quietly. "Ain't nothing I can do about that."

And she was right.

That mark stayed on my forehead for years. Decades, actually.

I was forty years old before that scar finally faded. Forty years of expensive creams, dermatologist visits, skin treatments, and scrubs before I could look in the mirror and not see Unk's cruelty staring back at me.

But even now, when the light hits my forehead just right, I can still see the faint shadow of it.

A reminder that some wounds take a lifetime to heal.

And some never do.

For us, losing a mother wasn't enough. Living with grief wasn't enough. Learning to survive in a house that wasn't ours wasn't enough.

We also had to survive each other.

And sometimes, that was the hardest part of all.

Weep What you Sow

That night, Fat-al got into trouble for me lying on him. He left and stayed a few days with our auntie because my grandmother didn't want people to see the marks on him. I tried to stay up, hoping he'd come back—back to Grandmother's house. It was my fault, and I didn't want to sleep until he did.

Guilt sat on my chest like a stone. I kept replaying the scene—my lie, his punishment, Grandma's rage, his words: "I wish my momma was living."

I do too, I thought. I wish she was here so none of this would be happening. So we could be home. So we could be us again.

My body felt warm lying close to Nickie. My eyes were heavy, but I fought off sleep.

Then—thump!

Pain hit my side.

"Oh no!" my auntie yelled. "Hoochy fell out of bed!"

I staggered toward her, zombie-like—I'd hit my head in the fall.

The room spun. Voices sounded far away. Someone's hands touched my face, tilted my chin, looked into my eyes.

"She alright?"

"Check for a bump—"

"Hoochy, how many fingers I'm holding up?"

"She look dazed—"

"Should we take her to the hospital?"

Hospital. That word again. The place where dead people go, where mothers don't come back.

"Sheritta, let her sleep with you so she won't fall again," my auntie said.

"I don't want her sleeping with me. She pees the bed," Sheritta complained.

The shame burned fresh. Even in my fog of pain and confusion, that rejection cut clear and deep.

As everybody rearranged, I squeezed into the bottom bunk near Sheritta's feet, lying head-to-toe with her. She kicked me. Hard. On purpose.

Her heel connected with my ribs. Once. Twice. A third time for good measure.

I cried, but nobody checked.

They'd all gone back to their rooms, their beds, their own problems. I was just Hoochy—the bed-wetter, the liar, the burden. The girl with the burn scar on her forehead that everyone would ask about for the next forty years.

The next morning, climbing out of the bottom bunk, I was still in pain. Sheritta noticed the knot on my shoulder—was it from the fall or the kick? She, the oldest, maybe felt guilty. As we dressed, she draped her favorite sweater over my shoulder, as if to hide it.

The sweater was soft, lavender, with small pearl buttons. Sheritta never let anyone wear her things. But that morning, she did. Gently. Without words.

It was the closest thing to an apology I'd get.

Downstairs, I gripped the rails for support. The screen door slammed over and over as everyone moved in and out. I slipped outside, unnoticed.

I looked across the street to Mom's house.

Why am I here? I live over there. I want to go home.

At the curb, my small head turned left, then right—just like I was taught. Cautious. Patient. Afraid. My mother's voice echoed in my head—the eyes in the back of my grandmother's head. Every step was watched. Every mistake remembered.

I scanned the street like my life depended on it—because it did. The sun bore down. Pavement hot. I wobbled, waiting for the traffic to clear.

Across the street, I saw Mom's house—657 Eliot. It might as well have been a mile away. I wanted to be there. That want was louder than fear, bigger than any past punishment.

So I waited, eyes darting, determined to cross.

But before I could step off the curb, a hand yanked me back by my right arm. I screamed in pain.

"Hoochy! Get your butt inside," Grandma shouted, her voice sharp with something I couldn't name then. Her anger pierced, but her eyes held a sadness she couldn't put into words. She didn't know how to show her fear, so it came out harshly.

That moment wasn't gentle, but it was real.

I didn't say a word. In the silence, a small flame lit inside me—anger, maybe, or heartbreak, or both. No one told me what was happening. No one asked how I felt. No one noticed I was hurt.

But the words stayed inside, for reasons I didn't understand.

I would hear "Hoochy!" morning and night. A year later, and I still hadn't gotten used to living with my grandmother. It was always the first sound, her voice cutting through the house like sirens.

The Days After the Nights

I keep starting it this way in my mind—"the day after"— even though the funeral was months away, not the next day. Memory doesn't care about timelines. It only cares about what broke you and when you first felt it.

Waking up–dark room.

So dark that sticks even after your eyes open.

I was in the top bunk, curled up beside Nickie. Sheritta was snoring on the bottom, her breath hitting the metal frame with each puff—rhythmic, steady, the only sound that felt normal.

The sheets were rough, worn thin from too many washes. The pillow was flat, offering nothing. My face was hot. My throat was tight, like I'd been crying in my sleep but couldn't remember.

And the auntie who held my hand the nights before?

She was gone. Just like Momma.

I didn't cry. Not yet. I just lay there, listening. Waiting for someone to say my name. Waiting for someone to check if I was awake, if I was okay, if I needed anything.

That's when I noticed it. Heavy. Wrapped in something stiff and hot. I moved, and it scratched my neck.

A cast.

They told me I broke my collarbone. I didn't recall how. Maybe I fell. Maybe I was pushed. Maybe it was Sheritta's kick from the bottom bunk.

The cast was hard and white, covered in names and scribbles pressed into it like graffiti on skin. I remember the markers squeaking as people signed—their voices careful and softly, like I might shatter if they said my name too loudly.

But time around then stopped making sense.

Days slid into each other. Mornings felt like the same long night. Hours disappeared into spaces I couldn't account for, leaving only fragments—a voice here, a touch there, faces that blurred together into one concerned expression.

I don't even remember him signing it.

I just remember looking down one day and seeing the words already there—

Love, Dad.

Crooked. Heavy-handed. Etched deep into the plaster, like someone wanted them to stay forever. As if permanence could replace presence.

I rubbed the letters with my thumb, trying to feel what I couldn't remember seeing. Trying to conjure the moment—his hand gripping the marker, his face bent close to mine, his voice saying something, anything, that would make those words real.

But there was nothing.

No picture of him holding the pen. No sound of his voice. No memory of him being there at all.

Just the words.

Two words that were supposed to mean everything but felt like nothing. A signature without a person. A claim without proof.

Love, Dad.

I traced those letters so many times that the plaster smoothed beneath my thumb. Like if I rubbed hard enough, I could erase them. Or make them true. I was never sure which I wanted more.

So many memories ended at 657 Eliot and then followed me across the street to 662.

The pain didn't belong to just one address—it unpacked itself there, too.

I wanted to believe. The week before, we lived on Eliot, we went to service, and the verse was Isaiah 41:10: "Fear thou not; for I am with thee."

That verse clung to me as we moved to a place I didn't know, a house I hadn't yet seen.

I also remembered Sunday school—the teacher's words about praying when we were hurt, confused, or angry.

She said God listens to children.

Psalm 127:3: "Behold, children are a blessing from the Lord; offspring of the earth, fruit of his belly."

So I prayed—and then I waited.

I waited.

Waited for someone to call me by my real name.

Waited for somebody to say I mattered.

Waited for a grown-up to look at me—not past me—and say, "You're going to be okay."

This was before school labeled me slow.

Before doctors whispered diagnoses.

Before they put me in a place for children with "special needs."

That name—my name—became my spine.

Not a curse. Not a joke.

But a sign that said, "You will survive this." And it wasn't just her death.

It was the silence that followed—a silence so loud it swallowed me.

I was never somebody's priority—just a name on someone's to-do list, a mouth to feed,
 A burden to shuffle. She's not my responsibility. That's what life taught me.

So I learned to be small—to shrink until I almost disappeared. I learned to observe, to read a room, to stay quiet. I learned that silence was safer.

In those early years, I built a wall inside myself. Brick by brick, anger held the pieces together.

Loneliness stacked them high. Confusion sealed it shut. But even in that house I was building in my soul,

God was already moving furniture around—making space. I just didn't know it yet.

I wanted to believe it meant something, that somewhere inside all this chaos, God was still teaching me how to stand.

The 2nd Burn

Rules couldn't protect us from everything.

Pearl tried—God knows she tried. But she was one woman raising multiple grandkids in a two-bedroom apartment, and she was tired. Bone-tired. The kind of tired that comes from decades of picking cotton, working factory lines, burying children, and refusing to break.

So sometimes, on Friday afternoons, she'd doze off on the couch while we played.

My young cousin, best friend, and trouble buddy. We were waiting for lunch: hot dogs boiling in a huge silver pot on the stove. My favorite.

"Hoochy, how do we know if they're done?" he asked.

"I don't know, let me see."

The stove was too high. I couldn't see into the pot—couldn't tell if the water was still bubbling or if the hot dogs were ready.

So, I did what seemed logical at the time: I pulled open the oven door and used it as a step.

"Hold on to me," I told my cousin, placing one hand on his shoulder for balance.

He was shorter than me, only four years old, but he tried. "Okay."

I stepped onto the oven door, reaching up toward the pot—

"Watch out!" he yelled, scrambling toward a chair.

The pot tipped.

Boiling water splashed across the stove, down the oven door, onto my feet. It hit the floor in a scalding wave, catching the back of my cousin's foot as he ran.

The pain was immediate—sharp, searing, unrelenting. Like something alive crawling under my skin, burning from the inside out.

I screamed.

Pearl jolted awake. "Hoochy, what did you do?"

My feet were on fire. The skin turned an angry red, then started to blister—fluid-filled bubbles swelling across both feet, shiny and wet and wrong.

I couldn't stop crying. My cousin was crying too, hopping on one foot, his heel blistering and raw.

Pearl's face went through a dozen emotions in seconds—fear, anger, worry, resignation.

She didn't take me to the hospital.

I didn't understand then, but I do now: I was a ward of the state. So was Nickie. So were the others. If Pearl took me to the emergency room with second-degree burns, they'd ask questions. They'd file a report. They'd decide she wasn't capable of keeping us safe.

And they'd take us.

Pearl had already lost my mother. She wasn't about to lose us —not to the system, not to foster care, not to strangers who didn't know our names or care about our stories.

So, she called the neighborhood doctor instead.

The one whose payment wasn't money.

I don't remember much about him—just hands that weren't gentle, a voice that wasn't kind, and Pearl turning her face away while he did whatever he did in exchange for treating my burns without paperwork.

What I do remember is the pain. Second-degree burns hurt badly, and mine throbbed for weeks. The blisters eventually burst, leaving raw, tender skin that stuck to my socks. Every step hurts. Every touch burned.

My cousin healed faster—his burn was minor, just the back of one heel.

But both of us learned something that day: even at 662, even with Pearl's rules and structure and Sunday dinners, we weren't safe. Not really.

Accidents happened. Pain happened. And sometimes, the people who loved you most had to make impossible choices—between protecting you and keeping you.

Pearl chose to keep us.

And I can't say if that was right or wrong. I just know it's what she did.

This wasn't the first time something had happened to one of us, and it wouldn't be the last. I'd already broken my collarbone. Nickie had been hit by a car. Fat-al busted his chin wide open.

We were Brewster kids, project kids, Black kids in Detroit in the late '70s and early '80s. Our childhoods were stitched together with near-misses and narrow escapes, held together by grandmothers who did the best they could with what they had.

And what they had was love.

Not the kind that prevents every injury or wipes away every tear or fixes every broken thing.

Just the kind that shows up. That stays. That refuses to let the state take you even when staying means risk.

That's the love Pearl gave us.

And for a long time, it was enough.

The Move to 558

AGES 6–7 — A NEW ADDRESS, THE SAME QUESTIONS FOR GOD

The following year, when we moved to 558 Wilkins in the South Brewsters, we landed next door to folks we used to live by on the North Side. Their setup mirrored ours— grandkids living with their grandmother because their mother's life was out of control. Drugs, men, mess. I didn't know their particulars, but I knew the picture. It looked a lot like mine.

"Good morning," I'd say to the two ladies on the shared concrete porch—same as ours, just mirrored on their side.

"Uhm," they'd reply, yanking their attention away, rolling an eyeball my way.

Our screen door creaked open. Nickie pulled the hard door closed with one hand and pushed through the screen, stepping onto the slab beside me.

I'd hear them say, "Hey, Nickie." Their whole bodies turned toward her, faces soft and smiling.

I knew then they hadn't just carried over their ugly-stepsister behavior from Eliot—they were bold enough to diss me right in front of my own sister.

"Forget y'all then," I said, giving them a long stare, trying to lock them in. They turned back around like they hadn't even heard me.

The South Side of the Brewsters was different—harder, faster, rougher. The buildings weren't clean; graffiti tagged them up. The drug activity was obvious. The playground wasn't always for play—it was a waiting zone for dealers. Heads darted left and right like a tennis match, ready to sprint the second a car or a cop came into view.

Older folks sat on milk crates outside the liquor store, smoking, drinking, talking trash, telling stories. The smell of piss baked into the bricks smacked your nose every time you turned the corner toward the store.

558 Wilkins was where I decided God wasn't fair to me... fair to us.

Pearl didn't talk about her pain. She cooked through it. Every morning, before the sun cracked the horizon, she was already up. Biscuits from scratch. Grits bubbling on the stove. Eggs scrambled with cheese if we were lucky, plain if we weren't. The kitchen was her war room, and breakfast was her battle cry.

She had raised four kids in a neighborhood that swallowed children whole. She watched her daughter— her beautiful, gifted, singing daughter—turn into a ghost with a needle in her arm.

And when Shanky died, Pearl didn't collapse. She didn't rage. She didn't abandon us.

She just... kept going.

But I know now—that wasn't strength without cost; it was a choice with consequences.

Pearl had every reason to be bitter. Every reason to let resentment harden her into stone. She could've looked at us—four more mouths, four more bodies, four more reasons her life would never be her own—and said, "No. I'm done."

But she didn't.

Instead, she woke up early. She ironed our church clothes even when the iron was broken and she had to heat it on the stove. She made sure we had food, even when the stamps ran out before the month did—and all we saw in the refrigerator was a silver ball of foil.

Every morning she'd call from the bottom of the stairs, "Y'all going to school today?" By then, I was enrolled at

Spain, and I hated school. So I'd shout back, "No!" or, "I don't know!" And she'd holler right back, "Well, you're getting the heck outta here anyway!"

She walked us to school with warm biscuits in our hands.

Pearl didn't have the words for therapy or healing. She had the rhythm of routine. The muscle memory of provision. She turned her grief into gospel—not the kind you sing, but the kind you live. That kind says: You will not go hungry. You will not be forgotten. You will survive this because I survived worse.

Her pain didn't disappear. I saw it flash hot when Fat-al talked back, when I ran toward traffic, when the bills piled up, and when Unk would hurt us. But she didn't let it sit. Didn't let it fester. She beat it into biscuit dough. Scrubbed it on the floors. Prayed it into silence at night when she thought we were all asleep.

She didn't sleep much. Washed our clothes with baking soda when the detergent ran out. Smashed roaches with her bare hands, like she was fighting back everything that tried to take us down.

She didn't poison us with her pain. She planted it. Watered it. And somehow, against all logic, against all odds— she grew from it.

That's what I didn't understand as a child. I thought she was just mean. Just strict. Just another person keeping me from what I wanted.

But Pearl wasn't trying to control me. She was trying to save me— from the same streets that took Shanky.

From the same spiral that starts with one bad choice and ends with a child standing at your funeral, wondering why you left.

Pearl chose us. Every single day. And that choice—quiet, unglamorous, exhausting—was faith in action, not the kind that shouts from a pulpit.

The kind that shows up at dawn and doesn't leave until the work is done.

Faith was in the house the whole time.

Pain Packed Itself into My Suitcase

We were living at 558 now, where pain unpacked its bags and decided to stay awhile.

Our church was still back in the North Brewsters, in the old neighborhood. Grandma didn't care about excuses—we were going. Sunday School was part of the routine, and honestly, I liked it a lot of the time. We had programs and activities, like an Easter egg hunt. I remember one Easter Sunday when the church gave us Easter speeches to take home and learn. My grandmother made us study harder than any homework at school.

I still remember a speech I gave called "Jesus Lives."

"Just because He loved us so"

Jesus died once long ago

But He rose on Easter Day

Now let all his children say

Jesus lives! Jesus Lives!

Oh, I'm happy! Jesus lives!

And yet, I kept thinking... but my mother was dead.

The church building was beautiful—stained glass windows and a red carpet flowing from the entry to the front of the sanctuary. The women dressed clean and sharp—big hats and flowing dresses. Men in three-piece suits and shiny shoes. Cleanliness as next to godliness—that's what it looked like on the outside. The inside? Who am I to say?

It was a Baptist church—Shiloh Baptist. A small congregation. Very formal. Very religious—acting, that is, like Nicodemus. Except for those two or three women whose dresses fit like they were sewn on. Tight and short, always up front, smiling at the Pastor. I didn't understand then why his wife looked back at them with the coldest glare. Then, after service, she'd kiss their cheeks, one side at a time. Behind their heads, she grinned, but as she pulled back toward their faces, she switched to a smile that looked like it was stitched on. Polite poison.

Now I know what that was about—like so many things, you only grasp when you get older and start reflecting. With age and wisdom comes understanding. The Bible. Proverbs. Solomon urges his son to seek understanding, when we moved to 558 Wilkins, that became my pursuit—to get understanding and wisdom.

How do I seek and understand a God who took my mother and called Himself my Father and Jesus my Savior? The anger and quiet I'd started using as my strength pushed me to rebel—to seek wisdom the only way a young kid knows how. That part comes later.

I wanted to know God's purpose for my life without parents. I wanted to know who would choose men and drugs over their own kids. I wanted to know how so many children are left with no mom, and yet our grandparents say God loves us. The Sunday School teacher and the preacher both say God loves us.

Most days I felt unloved and invisible. Like the world spun forward and I was stuck beneath it. I wasn't angry just to be angry. I was angry because it was the only thing that stayed. Emotions came and went, but anger? Anger sat with me. It didn't ask questions. It didn't leave. It filled the hollow parts when love couldn't reach them.

Abandonment doesn't show up all at once. It creeps in slowly, curling around your thoughts like smoke. As a child, I didn't have the vocabulary to call it abandonment. I just knew the silence after bedtime, the ache in my chest when no one said goodnight, the way my siblings looked at me when I tried to be strong.

I learned to listen—really listen—to the adults in my life, not because they always made sense, but because they carried pieces of the puzzle. Their whispers behind doors, the names they dropped mid-argument, the stories they didn't think I could hear—those became clues. I started to understand the weight of addiction, the lies of broken love, and the quiet way some people disappear without ever leaving the room.

558 was a bigger unit. We went from Grandma's two-bedroom spot to a four-bedroom one, big enough to fit all six of us. The setup was different—only three other doorways in our section. The units were shorter, tighter. We even had an overhead roof right outside my bedroom window. I'd stare out at the full moon, and sometimes I'd see my mother's face in it. Which ties back to a story my sister would tell.

Fewer than Two Years w/ Dad

For about a year, this was the routine: school, church, Dad's house. I was around seven, going on eight years old, starting to understand more. I could finally express myself a little better.

After church, my grandmother would sometimes let us visit our dad—which always felt strange, because I didn't remember him much before my mom's death. Meeting him for the first time at the funeral, introducing himself like that counted.

My aunt once told me a story about my dad, saying it wasn't his fault he wasn't around. I asked whose it was. She wouldn't say, but she told me he loved me and my brother very much, and he tried to stay.

So, was it Shanky's fault?

Do you notice I call her "Mom" when I'm dreaming of a woman who wanted me, loved me, chose me above all others? But when it's the pain and frustration and blank spaces I have to fill in, it's "Shanky," as if I could call her that to her face. I would get my head knocked off—based on the stories and the punishments I remember.

After Sunday School, we'd change out of our church clothes and head to his place near Woodward. He lived in a big four-unit building. My father, Gerald Lee, had served in the U.S. Army for years. He had health issues—maybe from the military, maybe from the drug life he'd also lived. I never asked. He never answered.

Sometimes my uncle—the one who gave me my nickname—would come by while we were there. It made sense; they were brothers. They'd sit, drink, talk, and sometimes he'd slide us a few dollars. They were the only two brothers I ever saw from their family because no one else came around. I heard my dad had three brothers, and his father lived in California with his wife, not my birth grandmother. I only saw Uncle Milton.

Before Uncle could hit the stoop, I'd run to meet him. He'd stop me mid-run, arm out like a cop directing traffic.

"No, ain't got no money, so don't even ask," he'd bark. The alcohol on his breath stopped me cold, kept me from getting near his face.

"I wasn't going to ask you for any money," I said, turning back toward the stairs, telling myself I didn't want anything from him—while my gut and heart debated who believed my mouth.

As we started going to my father's house each week, the building felt huge and creepy, almost haunted. The big concrete steps to the main door stretched long, and the door itself stood ten feet tall, heavy and solid. I could barely hold it open for my siblings because I always wanted to be first inside.

Entering the corridor, the floors shone in spots, with scuffs and skid streaks leading all the way to the back. My father lived on the first floor, likely because of his wheelchair, but the entry opened to a grand staircase curving upward. The banister was solid wood, and it became our slide whenever my father told us to step out while he had "special visitors."

These visitors were other men, tough-looking, always carrying black bags. They'd grin at us like the Grinch stealing Christmas.

I adored my dad. I don't know why. Maybe just because he was mine. He was my dad. That was enough for me.

My siblings didn't feel the same. Especially Sheritta and Nickie. Sheritta wasn't his child at all. And I think—maybe—he had doubts about Nickie too. But Fat-al (Gerald Jr.) and me? We looked like Washingtons. No denying it.

And for the first time in a long time, something empty in me started to fill. I had my dad. I had an uncle. I had pieces of family that felt like mine.

Then one Sunday, everything cracked again.

I was waiting by the window. My uncle had said he was coming to take me to see my dad. It had been a few Sundays—Dad was in the hospital. I didn't really understand why.

I waited. The sun went down. Night came up. And finally, my uncle showed.

I ran to the door, but my grandmother was already on the porch, talking to him. I could see his face through the window—faint sadness, dismay. I thought he was just sorry for being late.

"Bye, Nickie and Fat-al! I'm going with Uncle Milton!" I shouted, pushing the screen door open.

He was leaving again, already headed back toward his car, and I just exploded.

"No!" I yelled. "Where are you going? Wait for me!"

"You said I was going to see him today!"

My voice broke. My whole body broke. Tears shot out of me like fire as my grandmother blocked me with her arm.

"Hoochy, stop," she said.

My uncle turned, one hand on his car roof, the other holding his keys, his neck bent like it could barely hold up his head. The slow-motion effect took over, like back at Eliot. I flopped down on the porch as if gravity yanked me to the ground. My arms felt heavier than my legs, and I hit the slab so hard my hands clenched from the sting.

"He's not dead! You're wrong!" My voice trembled. "I hate everybody!" The words came out hard.

I was sobbing, screaming, breaking all at once. It wasn't just sadness. It was grief colliding with confusion. My heart broke, and I didn't have the right words. I just felt it.

My tears dried up instantly as a voice spoke inside: "I told you God doesn't love you." It was anger.

"Hoochy, I'm sorry... It's gonna be okay," my uncle said gently, stepping toward me, reaching for my shoulder.

I snatched away, eyes like lasers—Superman sharp, like I could cut you with a stare.

My grandmother whispered behind me: "Hoochy, your daddy wasn't right. He never was right by you kids."

Then a voice from deeper in the house—I don't even know whose—snapped, "Hoochy, cut it out."

But how could I?

Anger spoke again: "I got you. You don't need them."

My face split in two like Two-Face from DC Comics—the left side grinning with hate stretched to my ear; the right side thinking hard about how I'd never come to God, how I'd prove He wasn't loving.

That night, after everyone went to bed, I sat on the floor in the dark corner of the room I shared with my sisters. Knees pulled to my chest, arms wrapped tight. And I talked to God—or at Him, really. At Him.

"You took my mama," I whispered, voice raw and cracked. "And now You took my daddy too. Before I even got to know him right."

I wiped my face with the back of my hand.

"Everybody says You love children. That You hear us. But You don't hear me. You never did."

My throat tightened, and the words came faster, meaner.

"I hate You. I hate that I ever believed in You. I hate that I thought You cared."

I sat there in the silence, waiting for something—lightning, a voice, a feeling. Anything.

But there was nothing. Just my cousins breathing in their sleep and the hum of the refrigerator down the hall.

And that's nothing? That silence? It felt like proof.

God didn't love me. He never had. And I was done waiting for Him to show up.

That night, I decided God hated me. Life was never going to be fair. And I was never going to love anybody again.

After a few days of nursing my new emotions, what my grandmother said about my father proved true—and the familiar rhythm started again. Strangers come in and out of our house. Another stream of footsteps. More faces I didn't know. More food. More tears. More murmurs.

This time, I was sitting outside 558 Wilkins—but it felt like 662 Eliot all over again.

So many memories ended with Eliot and followed me to 558. The pain didn't belong to just one address—it unpacked itself at two.

Jerry Reflection

THE FATHER WHO EXISTED IN GLIMPSES AND VEINS

Jerry to some. Gerald Lee Washington to the military. To me—for two whole years—he was just... Dad.

Yes, I said it—Dad. Not because he lived with us or walked us to school or taught me to ride a bike. He never tucked me in. Never coached a team. Never pulled me close just to say he loved me.

But he was mine. MY father. And in a world where so many things about me felt like question marks, that felt like a period. I knew he was mine. Unlike my sisters— whose fathers were more mystery than memory, more rumor than reality—my father had a name. A face. And for two years, he gave me something close to an answer.

He lived in a towering two-story brick building—not the Brewsters, but close enough for me to walk to his place every Sunday after church. Far enough, though, that at six I thought he was rich. The wide sidewalk on his block looked like something out of a storybook. Not the princess kind—no ballgowns, no glass slippers—but the dark, enchanted kind. It reminded me of Beauty and the Beast, the way Belle walks toward the Beast's castle: afraid, curious, unsure.

That was me. Small feet, big steps, in front of what felt like a mansion with ten-foot doors that groaned when we pushed them open. The kind of doors you had to put your whole back into. Inside, the stairwell curved up like it was trying to touch heaven—and every step toward his apartment felt like a step deeper into my own identity. The hallway was long and narrow, with just one other door past his. Creepy and quiet. I never went down it, but my brother did. And it cost him. Big.

Jerry's door? Old brass knob, barely held by a single screw. When we turned it, it wobbled like it was warning him someone was coming. Maybe that was on purpose. Maybe it was his way of staying in control of something.

We pushed it open—me, Nicole, and Sheritta together—and there he was.

Always the same spot. Always the same look. Hair combed from back to front, glasses thick as magnifying lenses—we used to call them "Coke bottles" and laugh—behind his back. Never to his face.

His clothes never changed—dark pants, a dingy shirt. The room stayed dim, smoky, quiet. And even in his illness—even in that wheelchair, that feeble body—I didn't see weakness. When he spoke, his voice was deep. Demanding. He didn't move much, but when he talked, you listened.

What I saw in that room wasn't just a sick man. I saw pain. I saw hurt. I saw something else too—an unnamed emotion. And in him, like a mirror, I recognized my own identity—etched in the features we shared, and in the way pain sat on him, in his demeanor, his countenance.

Jerry–MY father. Tall in pictures. Slim, with huge feet, Uncle Milton once said he was 6'2". But I never saw that man. The one I knew? Wheelchair-bound. Mostly in bed. Always the same clothes—dingy shirt, dark pants.

No matter when we visited, the room was dark and smoky, the air was thick with dust and silence. And it smelled... like something had given up.

He wasn't a good father. But he was present... for a while. And in a neighborhood where girls like me were teased—"You don't even got no daddy!"—I'd clench my teeth and ball my fists and think: But I do.

And when I looked at Jerry, I saw pieces of myself. Not just reflections. Proof.

You know how some kids come out looking exactly like one parent? Sheritta looked like our mom. Some siblings are a split—top half one, bottom half the other. But me? I was a patchwork quilt of DNA. Mama's face shape. Daddy's chin. Mama's eyes, Daddy's eyeballs—huge and soft. Mama's nose, but the length? Grandma's. My daddy's hairline with Shanky's forehead. Like God took both of them, broke them into puzzle pieces, and said, "Let's see what happens."

I wasn't pretty. But I wasn't ugly either. Some days, I'd look in the mirror and find moments of beauty. Glimpses of her. Traces of him. Mostly, though, I'd look and ask God the same question I always did: "Why?"

Jerry helped answer that. In small ways. In quiet ones. A familiarity I didn't have words for. Even if all he ever did was look at me like he knew I was his.

If Shanky's shadow stretched over my life loud and wild, Jerry's was quiet. Thin. Almost see-through. The kind of shadow a man casts when he's only half in the world and halfway gone–With her I felt forgotten.

With him, I felt connected.

I'm Not My Hair—Nor My Siblings
AGES 8 — LEARNING TO SEE MYSELF BEYOND WHAT I WAS TOLD

People see pieces of you reflected in your parents and think they know your story. They clock your skin, your hair, your last name—and decide who you are.

I learned later I'm not what you see. I'm not my family's mistakes, my mom's shadow, or their favorites. I'm the space between all that—less what you can see than what you can't, a land held together by my faith.

When you look back at your life—the good, the bad, the ugly—those memories, cut up, make a truer picture of what really was.

Even now, as I write, childhood memories flood back. Some make me smile as I type; others hit so hard it's a gut-wrenching pain shooting through my chest. Tears build. My jaw clamps tight.

Take my mom or auntie—at Spain, back when it was called Lincoln. They had a teacher named Mr. Kidd, and boy, did he love my mom, my oldest sister, and Nickie. Maybe because they behaved. Maybe because they were beautiful.

Fat-al and I were the troubled kids—the ones teachers warned each other about. Every year started the same: "I hope you're like your sisters. They were such good students."

I was compared to Nickie so much—especially how I looked—that I started dressing like Fat-al, like a boy. Easier that way. I could hide inside toughness.

One Christmas, I asked for a Ken doll, a G.I. Joe, a Stretch Armstrong. Instead, I got a Barbie—a knockoff Black Barbie. Brown like me. Hair only on top. Long neck, a thin red line for lips, a head that popped off at the slightest twist.

I remember thinking, "She looks just like me—easy to break, hard to love."

Those were the days when girls hot-pressed their hair. I can still smell the fried grease every Monday when my classmates came back—foreheads shining, parts laid just right, bangs flipped high for the girls lucky enough to have hair to flip.

Not me anymore—especially after what Unk did to me. I wore mine tight, drawn-up, rigid, kinky, natural—like it had been holding its breath all weekend.

Most girls who didn't have pressed bangs had chemicals instead—Jeri curls, dripping. If you don't know what that is, go watch Coming to America or Next Friday. When you see Pinky—that's what I mean. Activator so thick it left a trail wherever they went. You could smell them before you saw them.

The boys looked the same—glossy, dripping, "pretty."

As much as I hated those greasy curls, I wanted them—the swing, the shine, the smell of pretty. Just not the mess that came with it.

To go swimming with a Jeri curl, you had to wrap your head like a Thanksgiving turkey—two shower caps and a swim cap on top.

Me? I didn't have that problem. I could jump right in, splash around, and climb out the same way I went in. My hair wasn't getting any more drawn-up or nappier than it already was.

Freedom came in its own way.

I hated school. They labeled me slow. Special. Too angry. Too distracted.

But how could I focus? My mom was dead. My house was chaos. My name was Hoochy.

I fought. Fought other girls. Fought teachers. Fought myself.

At school, it only got worse.

I talked back to teachers. Not because I was stupid—I knew the answers. I just didn't like how they asked. Didn't like the tone. Didn't like being told what to do by people who didn't even know my name the week before.

I threw a book once. Not at anyone. Just across the room.

The teacher asked why, and I had no answer. I just knew something in me needed to move, to break the stillness, to prove I was still alive under all that quiet.

They sent me to the principal's office. They called my grandmother. Pearl came, tight-lipped and stiff-shouldered, and didn't say a word to me the whole walk home.

When we got back, she sat me down.

"You think you grown?" she asked.

I didn't answer.

"You think because your mama gone you can act any kind of way?"

I still didn't answer. Truth was—I didn't know what I thought. I just knew I was angry, with nowhere to put it except out into the world around me.

I pushed. I tested. I broke small rules just to see if anyone cared enough to stop me.

And when they did stop me—with belts, with timeouts, with Jackson, with silence—I pushed harder. Because at least when I was being punished, I was being seen.

What I didn't understand then was that God was shaping me through the fight—forming the part of Hoochy who would one day cry out to Him. He was already my Father, but He needed me to call His name.

She Saw Past My Name

Thinking back, in the third grade was also when I started figuring out who I was—when I realized the person who saw me clearly wasn't at church or at home. It was my third-grade teacher.

I used to get in trouble every single day in Ms. H class. The rule was simple: if your name went up on the board and stayed up till Friday, you couldn't go to gym.

Every Friday, Jule, Yvonne, and I were stuck in our chairs while the rest of the class ran off to play. I'd watch them line up at the door, bouncing on their toes, buzzing with excitement. As they left, a few would look back and snicker, whispering just loud enough for me to hear.

"Hoochy in trouble again."

"She never gets to go."

I'd slump down, arms crossed, face hot. I wasn't sad—I was mad. Mad at them for laughing. Mad at myself for caring.

The fluorescent lights flickered overhead as Ms. H planted herself next to my desk, her shadow slicing across my notebook. Her crisp blazer was buttoned tight; the lines around her eyes said she'd fought more than a few classroom battles. "Hoochy—" she started, then caught herself. "Yolanda," she said, her tone a mix of skepticism and something almost like hope. "I bet you can't behave for more than a week."

I looked up at her. My jaw tightened.

"What you mean, you bet?" I said, my voice sharp.

"I mean exactly that. I don't think you can do it. Prove me wrong."

Something about that word—bet—lit a spark. It wasn't a punishment. It wasn't a threat. It was a challenge. And I didn't back down from those.

I stood up straight, arms stiff at my sides, chin high.

"I bet *chew* I can."

She smiled. Not a mean smile. A knowing one.

"Alright then. Let's see."

She psyched me out, an eight-year-old with more anger than sense—but she planted something. That was the first time I realized that even if no one else believed in me, I could still bet on myself.

That challenge didn't just make me behave for a week. It started shaping the fighter in me.

I made it through Monday. Tuesday. Wednesday without a mark. By Thursday, kids were staring at me like I'd grown a second head.

By Friday, my name wasn't on the board.

Ms. H walked past my desk and tapped it twice with her knuckles.

"Told you," I said, grinning.

"You told me," She corrected. "Now do it again next week."

And I did. Not because I was suddenly good. But because I wanted to win.

When Six Fell to Five.

I came home from school one afternoon, still riding the high of keeping my name off the board. But the house felt different—quieter, heavier.

Sheritta's stuff was gone.

Her bed was stripped. Her clothes weren't piled in the corner anymore. The space where she slept looked hollow, like a tooth knocked out.

"Where's Sheritta?" I asked, dropping my backpack by the door.

No one answered.

"Where'd she go?"

Grandma was in the kitchen, stirring something on the stove. Her back was to me, shoulders tight.

"She left," Grandma said flatly.

"Left where?"

"Just left, Hoochy. Don't ask me about it."

I looked at Nickie. She shrugged. Fat-al didn't even look up.

No one explained why. No one said she was coming back. No one said goodbye.

Grandma always said, "Shanky's kids stay together." She said it so many times I thought it was written somewhere—like in the Bible or the law.

But we didn't stay together.

That day felt like thunder in the middle of summer—no warning, just noise that split the air. Then came the silence—the kind that meant something broke, and nobody was going to fix it.

My oldest sister, Sheritta, left us at thirteen. Left me at 9.

Maybe I already knew she would. Her daddy wasn't mine. She was lighter, softer, prettier. Back then, light skin was in.

I knew it because I was crazy for El DeBarge—slim build, good hair that didn't even need activator, smooth voice. My sister looked like she belonged in his video. She had more hair than Nickie and me combined. She could flip her bangs. And for a while, she wore the Jheri curl— that's how her hair got long.

Back home, Nickie and I caught it from both sides— called names, picked on, pushed aside. Bald head wasn't because my hair was cut; it was short, coiled tight—what they now call "natural." Back then, it just meant poor.

Later, I saw a study that said white dolls were preferred over dark-skinned dolls among black girls.

What does that say?

Favoritism is a quiet kind of violence. It's when love shows up for one person and forgets to call your name. The oldest got it all—attention, affection, protection— even when she didn't ask for it.

Don't get me wrong: she didn't move far—just far enough to find her own trouble. While Nickie and I were getting called names and picked on, she was finding a new kind of pain, a new resentment. Her anger was building, just like mine.

Her anger showed—the downward brows, the quick, snatchy way she'd take things from us, the rough pull of my clothes, dragging me any which way just to shove me out of her path. That green vein down the center of her forehead showed me what burden looked like, pulsing with everything she couldn't say.

But I can't lie—she took care of me when I was little. Kept me fed and warm back at 657. She told me she was my mother, since Shanky was too busy being somebody else's friend, too busy chasing her own choice.

And I believed her. Because when you're hungry for love, even broken love feels like a meal.

Before middle school, before Mr. Flood—I had a teacher's aide who used to pull me out of class. I thought it was for handwriting lessons, but then I noticed the other kids—they struggled to speak, read, and stay calm. Some couldn't handle second-grade books.

At first, I loved leaving math and English to go there. The work was easy, and I was always the first to finish. The other kids thought I was smart, asking me for help.

Then one day, I raised my hand.

"Why am I in this class?"

The teacher smiled softly. "Yolanda, everyone here has some kind of learning disability. They placed you here based on your test scores."

"Oh heck naw!" I shouted, storming out the door.

The other kids yelled out my name—"Yolanda!" "Hoochy!"—some screaming just to scream, some begging me not to leave. They didn't know what I was running from.

But those kids—my "special class"—I ended up defending them. Protecting them. I became their voice when others laughed or mocked them.

If you were Hoochy's friend, no one messed with you.

I fought for them because I understood them—the tics, the sounds, the flailing hands. I could calm them down.

"Mikey, I know James took your pencils. Calm down," I'd whisper, then sing softly, "Jesus loves me, this I know..." until his breathing slowed. That was my Soft Kitty moment long before Sheldon ever said it on TV.

Similar, Not the Same

Fat-al was in and out of the house, mostly out from thirteen on. He found his love in sports—good at every game you could name and born understanding the numbers.

Fat-al was Jerry, just shorter and thicker in later years. Back then, he was so skinny, my grandmother used to threaten him when he got in trouble, saying, "Boy, I'm gonna choke your skinny chicken neck if you keep on."

He got picked on in the streets and at home, too. It was as if the family had already written his story—like his destiny was to fall—and so he did. He left home, started selling drugs, and came back only when the streets spit him right back out. Sometimes we'd sneak him in through the downstairs window. In the morning, Grandma—who hadn't seen him in months—would wake up to find him sleeping on our floor.

His shine broke when our parents died. His identity left with Jerry. Fat-al—like the show—was born April 27th, in Detroit, Michigan, in the arms of both our parents. He was their first, and soon after, they got married. Back then, if you weren't married, the child couldn't take the father's last name. So even though most of his school records listed him as Gerald Washington, his birth certificate listed him as Carr. Another strike against his spirit and identity.

Fat-al and I looked alike. We laughed alike. We carried the same mischief and humor. I adored my brother, and I miss him dearly—he passed away in 2007. I didn't mind being compared to him; most times when I was, it was because we were both in trouble.

My sisters, though? Never. The only comparison I got to them was hair or skin tone. People swore Nickie and I looked alike, but I could never see it.

Nickie had these big cheeks—like two little apples hiding on each side of her face. Her nose was thin, her lips small—no, gone—and her eyes, brown and cat-slanted, made her look soft and sweet even when she wasn't.

Her forehead was less than a four—yeah, that's when you hold up four fingers to measure across your head. If it fits, that's a "natural forehead."

Me? I had five heads. My hairline was so far back it caught the 4 p.m. bus while I was still on the 10 a.m. school bus.

My looks were split between my parents, though I never saw much of either in my own face. Maybe Grandma.

I had thick lips, a medium nose, eyes big and wide with a slight slant at the ends—brown eyes that seemed to shift shades with my moods. My best feature, I'd say, was my eyebrows—naturally arched and full, nothing like Nickie's, which were thin and missing in spots like Grandma's.

There was beauty and ugliness in all of us, but mine always came with a fight. I had to learn to see it—to find it somewhere between the nappy curls, the hand-me-down clothes, and the world that said I wasn't enough.

Maybe that's why I clung to humor—teasing and laughter—because sometimes it was the only thing that made the mirror feel like mercy.

Curb Ball

AGE 9-10 — WHEN LIFE STARTED THROWING HARD LESSONS MY WAY

In the moments when life seemed to shine and offer me some comfort, it was always when I was outside the house. Even now, living in the South End of the Brewsters, I could still find joy.

Summer gave us breathing room. There were ice cream trucks rolling through the streets, kids screaming for change. The fire hydrants turned on — illegally, of course — spraying water over cracked concrete, turning sidewalks into splash pads, cooling us off from the dry heat.

The playground came alive—team sports on Brewster Field, the indoor pool, free lunch at the Brewster Center.

And most importantly: no school.

I saw my school friends, and we invented games out of nothing. Double dutch. Hopscotch. Freeze tag.

But the game that defined those summers—our own ghetto Olympics—was curb ball.

Unless you grew up in the projects, you probably don't know curb ball—it wasn't just bouncing a ball around.

You needed curbs spaced just right—far enough for a car to squeeze through, close enough to throw from one side and clip the opposite curb with skill. Hit the very top edge and the ball snapped back to you. That meant a point. And another turn.

But if the ball dropped too low and the person on the other curb caught it, that was no points. Your turn was over. Street law.

I remember one hot day like it was yesterday.

The sun had been beating down since morning, softening the asphalt under my sneakers. The kind of heat that made air shimmer above parked cars and left sweat trickling down the back of my neck. My T-shirt stuck to my shoulder blades. The rubber ball felt slick in my palms—warm from sitting in the sun between rounds.

I was playing curb ball with Belinda—my friend my age. Black like me, poor like me. But there was one difference.

She had long hair. Down to her shoulders.

Now you might be asking why that even matters. But you know what they used to call me and my sister? The bald-head sisters. Not because we had no hair, but because it was short. Nappy. The kind of hair people judged back then—now they pay to imitate. Funny how life flips the script.

That day, Belinda and I were outside my house on Wilkins, laughing, sweating, talking junk, throwing that ball. In case you don't know, "talking junk" means bragging or boasting—talking smack. It was a form of joy. Black girl joy.

The smell of somebody's barbecue drifted from a few houses down—ribs or chicken, I couldn't tell which. My stomach growled even though I'd eaten lunch at the Brewster Center not two hours before. Mrs. Jackson's radio played the Isley Brothers from her open window. Someone's baby cried in the distance, then stopped. Life moved around us while we played.

Hoochy: 6 points. Belinda: 5 points. Winner at 10.

I bent my knees, brow furrowed. I locked onto the curb across the street, replaying my last hit. My right arm swung back like a slingshot. I tried to recreate the perfect throw. I didn't blink—I needed this bounce.

The ball shot forward, full force—at least as much force as girl weighing sixty pounds could muster. My chin lifted, eyes tracking the ball.

But something shifted.

Belinda's feet were still planted on the opposite curb. But next to her—another pair of feet.

Beaten-up shoes.

Brown, baggy pants. No belt. A white T-shirt.

My eyes followed the shape upward.

Before I could fully process who it was—BANG!

The ball smacked me square in the face. Right between the eyes. My nose stung. My head snapped back and I landed on my butt, palms smacking the pavement.

Tiny pebbles pressed into my skin. The metallic taste of blood touched my tongue—I must've bitten the inside of my cheek when I fell. My eyes watered, not from crying but from the shock of impact. The world tilted for a second, sounds muffled like I was underwater.

My head throbbed. But that wasn't what shook me.

It was him.

That face. That frame.

Suddenly, I was five again. Standing in the hallway. And that same man was standing over my momma's body.

One word clawed its way out of my throat:

"George!"

As I stood up, my thoughts scattered. My sense of smell and time vanished. This had to be a dream—even though my nose still burned where the ball had smacked me.

My vision worked because George started walking toward me.

His shadow stretched long across the pavement, reaching me before he did. Each step deliberate. Not rushed. Like he had all the time in the world. Like he belonged here.

"Hello, Hoochy. Do you remember me?" he said.

His voice—I remembered that voice. Low and raspy, like gravel scraping concrete. The kind of voice that had probably sweet-talked my momma a hundred times. The kind that probably lied just as often.

I stared up at this sandy-complexioned man with short curly hair and a thin mustache, like he'd trimmed it days ago. He carried a worn-out gym bag—hugged it to his chest like it held everything he owned. Clutching the strap with his left hand, even though the handle was thrown over his right shoulder.

His eyes were bloodshot. Red lines spider-webbing through the whites. Either he'd been crying or drinking or hadn't slept in days. Maybe all three. His lips were dry, cracked at the corners. When he smiled—and he did smile, a thin, uncertain thing—I saw a missing tooth on the left side.

The smell hit me then. Stale cigarettes. Old sweat. Something sour underneath, like milk gone bad. The smell of someone who'd been sleeping in their clothes. Who didn't have a place to wash up properly. Who'd been on the streets too long.

Back up, Hoochy.

Run, fool.

Move, fool.

I could hear Belinda's voice in the background, like she was thirty feet away, even though she'd been right across the street seconds ago.

"Hoochy, are you okay? Who is that?! Run! He's coming!"

Belinda took off in the opposite direction as she yelled. Her footsteps slapped the pavement, fading fast. Smart girl. She knew danger when she saw it, even if she didn't know the whole story.

Finally, my body had a conversation with my feet:

Get your butt moving.

And just like that, my legs listened.

I backed up first. Still staring at him. Still unsure if fear or anger or confusion was steering me. My body turned to run, but my face hadn't looked away. Part of me still needed to confirm what I saw—as if turning fully might make it more real.

George's face changed. His smile dropped. His eyebrows squeezed together—was that disappointment, hurt, or something darker, something that resembled need. "Wait—" he started, reaching one hand toward me.

I bolted.

Straight for the house. The door was always unlocked.

My feet pounded up the steps. Two at a time. The screen door banged behind me—the sound echoing through the empty living room. No one home. Just me and the ghosts of everything that had happened in this place.

Straight to my room.

I didn't look back.

I slammed the door and hit the bed. But it wasn't safety I felt. It was rage.

My heart hammered so hard I felt it in my throat. My hands shook. I pressed them flat against my thighs to stop the trembling. My nose still throbbed where the ball had hit me. I touched it gently—tender but not broken.

The room smelled like old carpet and the faint mildew that lived in the corners we couldn't quite clean. Afternoon light slid through thin curtains, turning everything pale yellow. Dust motes floated in the air, stirred up by my rush.

I sat there listening. Listening for footsteps on the porch. Listening for the door to open. Listening for his voice calling my name.

But there was nothing. Just the distant sound of someone's music. A car passing. Kids still playing somewhere down the block.

That day, my anger grew three sizes—like the Grinch's heart, but in reverse. My heart didn't grow. It shrank.

My wall got higher.

My silence deepened.

I wasn't just afraid of men—I started hating them.

I wasn't just confused about God—I decided He had nothing worth saying.

And worst of all, I started hating myself. Not on the surface. Not in ways people could see. But in the places where little girls are supposed to dream, I only built prisons.

That was the day a part of me broke off and never came back.

George didn't touch me that day. But he didn't have to. His shadow walked straight into my house. And stayed.

From that day on, I became hyper-aware. Every man who walked past our house got watched. Every stranger who lingered too long got memorized—face, clothes, walk, voice. I learned to read body language the way some kids learn to read books. I learned when to run, when to hide, when to pretend I didn't exist.

Nobody told me this was what little girls were supposed to learn. Nobody said, "Hoochy, here's how you protect yourself when the adults can't." But I learned anyway. Because I had to.

Nickie and I were now the only two left in the house with my grandmother. Sometimes our cousins or other relatives would visit and stay a few days, but day-to-day reality? That was just us.

The Streetlight Rules:

Nickie was a teenager now, and the good girl was slipping into bad things. Missing curfew. Out with boys. Running with friends who didn't care about porches or sundown. She wanted out of 558 Wilkins—out of that house, that life.

In the projects, streetlights were the law. When those orange bulbs flickered on, stretching long shadows across cracked pavement, that was your signal. Time's up. Get home. No exceptions.

"When them lights come on, your behind better be on this porch!" Grandma would yell from the doorway, her voice carrying down the block.

Every grandmother said it. Every mother. It wasn't a suggestion—it was a command backed by a switch, a belt, or worse: disappointment.

The streetlights meant safety, in theory. Meant you weren't out there when the real darkness fell—not just the kind that came from the sun going down, but the kind that came with it. The dealers posting up on corners. The dice games that turned into fights. The cars that rolled through slow, windows down, eyes hunting for trouble or opportunity.

But Nickie didn't care about streetlights anymore. She'd come home when the sky was pitch black, smelling like cheap perfume and cigarette smoke that wasn't hers. She'd slip through the door trying to be quiet, but Grandma always knew.

"Where you been?" Grandma would demand, already working herself up.

"Out," Nickie would say. Just that. Nothing more.

And what could Grandma do? She was tired. Old. Fighting her own demons in a mayonnaise jar. The rules she'd raised us with—the ones that kept her children alive in Detroit, the ones that got her through the Depression and the war—no longer held the same weight.

Nickie was slipping away, and we both knew it.

My grandmother didn't want her to leave, but she couldn't control Nickie anymore. Not really. And not me either—at least not all the time.

I watched Nickie test boundaries, staying out later and later. I watched her eyes get that distant look—the exact look I'd seen in Momma's before everything fell apart. It terrified me.

Still, I wasn't leaving, not without Grandma.

I'd made that decision somewhere deep inside, in a place I couldn't explain. Maybe because I'd already lost Momma. Maybe because I knew what abandonment felt like. Maybe because underneath all the beer and the anger and the thrown objects, Grandma was still the steadiest thing I had.

Or maybe I was just too afraid to find out what happens to girls like me when they have nowhere else to go.

There were times I tried.

One day, my grandmother got drunk and threw an iron at my head—the last straw.

I had just gotten in from playing, hanging with friends outside, when my grandmother began stomping back and forth from the kitchen to the front door, mumbling, "Leave Fat-al alone. Leave Hoochy alone."

Her footsteps were heavy, uneven. The floorboards groaned under her weight. She moved in that particular way drunk people move—too careful with some steps, careless with others. Her housecoat flapped open, revealing the slip underneath. Her hair, usually neat, stood in wild tufts where she'd been pulling at it.

I never knew who she was speaking to, but I said, "Grandma, I'm okay."

Wrong time to interrupt her conversation with whoever.

She turned toward me, stopped dead. Her eyes were glazed, unfocused. Her face twisted into something I didn't recognize—not my grandmother's face, but the face of someone fighting invisible demons. Her jaw clenched. Spit gathered at the corners of her mouth.

I didn't realize something was about to fly. I turned to face her as I started up the stairs.

Like the Matrix, I moved slowly but fast enough to duck as a full clothes iron came flying toward me, cord and all.

The iron whistled through the air—I heard it. A whoosh, then the slap of the cord snapping behind it. It missed my head by inches and crashed into the wall with a heavy thunk. A chunk of plaster cracked and fell. The iron bounced once, twice, then settled with the hot plate facing up, still radiating heat even though it wasn't plugged in.

My ears rang. My scalp tingled where the iron had nearly connected. If I'd been a second slower, if my reflexes hadn't kicked in, it would've split my skull open.

"What the hell is wrong with you?" I said, forgetting who I was speaking to—and not caring.

My voice came out louder than I intended. Raw. Shaking with adrenaline and rage and something else—grief, maybe. Grief for whom my grandmother used to be before the beer swallowed her whole.

Before I could finish, she had already headed back to the kitchen. Back to the sink, that beer-filled mayonnaise jar going to her lips. Then she wandered into the living room again.

"Hoochy, I'm sorry," she said. "Grandma loves you."

She smiled like she'd forgotten she'd almost taken my life.

The smile was wrong. Too wide. Too empty. Like a mask someone puts on when they can't remember what happiness is supposed to look like. Her eyes were wet—tears or just the glassiness of too much drink; I couldn't tell.

She reached for me. I flinched back.

That's when I saw it—a flicker of recognition in her face. The moment she realized what she'd done. But it passed as quickly as it came, replaced by that vacant smile.

Nickie came to the top of the stairs. "What happened? What she do?"

Her voice was tight with fear. She gripped the banister with both hands, knuckles white against her dark skin. Her eyes darted between me and Grandma, calculating. Planning her next move if she needed to intervene.

Nickie had been the victim of Pearl's rants plenty of times. She knew how to stay upstairs.

I told Nickie, "I don't care if you're staying—I'm leaving this time."

In that moment, I understood something: even the rules of the outside—curfew, streetlights, porches—couldn't protect us from what waited inside. The street had its dangers, sure. But what lived beyond our own front door was its own kind of threat. We were caught between running away and staying to keep the light on for someone we loved, even when that someone hurt us.

The streetlights could tell you when to come home. They couldn't tell you what to do when home was the most dangerous place of all.

She followed me. We both left the house, but we didn't make it far. My sister came and got us.

Sheritta, now about sixteen, had a car. She was living with Auntie J. and doing well. School, life, stability—all the things we didn't have.

When she pulled up, her car was clean. Not new but washed. The interior didn't smell like beer, roaches, or decay. It smelled like air freshener—vanilla or something floral. She looked put together. Hair done. Clothes that fit. Lip gloss catches the light.

She looked at us through the windshield before we even got in—really looked. I saw something cross her face. Pity, maybe. Or guilt. Or relief that she wasn't us anymore.

And here comes "Hoochy" again—starting trouble, needing help, pulling people back into the chaos they tried to escape.

At that point, Sheritta didn't feel like my sister anymore. She was that high-yellow girl who left us. Left me. Left Nickie. Left Fat-al.

All we had was each other when my momma died.

And she left.

I climbed into the backseat without saying a word. Nickie took the front. The leather was hot against my bare legs—scorching from sitting in the sun. I shifted, uncomfortable in more ways than one.

Sheritta didn't ask what happened. Maybe she didn't need to. Maybe our faces said enough.

She put the car in drive, but before we could pull away, something in me snapped.

"So you just gonna act like you care now?" The words came out before I could catch them.

Sheritta's eyes flicked to the rearview mirror and met mine. "Excuse me?"

"You heard me." I leaned forward between the seats. "Where were you? Where you been?"

"Hoochy, don't start—" Nickie began, but I cut her off.

"Nah., she get to leave. Get to have a whole different life while we're stuck here with—" I gestured toward the house behind us. "With that? And now she wanna swoop in like she's rescuing us?"

Sheritta's jaw tightened. Her hands gripped the steering wheel harder. "And you don't know anything about what we've been through!" My voice cracked. Hot tears pricked my eyes, but I refused to let them fall. "You left us!"

"I was a kid too!" Sheritta twisted in her seat to face me. Her lip gloss couldn't hide the way her mouth trembled. "You think I wanted to leave? You think that was easy?"—you don't know what I've been through either!"

"Yeah, I do. I think it was really easy for you to go live your nice life while we—"

"Get out of the car." Her voice was ice.

"What?"

"Get. Out. The. Car." Each word sharp as broken glass.

"Sheritta—" Nickie tried again.

But I was already opening the door. Already stepping back onto the hot pavement. My pride burned hotter than the asphalt under my sneakers.

"Fine. I don't need you anyway."

Sheritta got out too. Slammed her door hard enough to make the whole car shake.

We faced each other across the roof—her on the driver's side, me on the passenger side. The metal burned under my palms where I gripped the door frame.

"You wanna say that again?" Her eyes were hard. Not the eyes of the sister I remember. Eyes that had learned to protect themselves. Eyes that had built their own walls.

"I said I don't need you. Never did."

She came around the car fast. Faster than I expected for somebody in platform sandals.

I should've backed up. Should've walked away. But I was tired of backing up. Tired of walking away. Tired of being the one left behind.

So, I stood my ground.

She got in my face—close enough that I could smell her perfume, something sweet and expensive girls from the projects couldn't afford unless somebody bought it for them.

"You don't know nothing," she hissed. "Nothing about what it took for me to get out. What I had to do. What I had to—" She stopped herself. Swallowed hard.

"Then tell me!" I shoved her shoulder. Not hard. Just enough.

It was enough.

She shoved me back. Harder. I stumbled but didn't fall.

"Don't put your hands on me, Hoochy."

"Or what? You gonna leave again?"

Her hand shot up—caught my shoulder, pushed me backward. I swung back, my fist glancing off her arm. We weren't really fighting. Not yet. Just going, grabbing, all that rage between us, trying to find somewhere to land.

She was bigger. Stronger. Older. She got the best of me quick—grabbed both my wrists, held them tight enough to hurt.

"Stop!" she yelled in my face.

But I didn't want to stop. Didn't want this to be over. Because as long as we were fighting, I could pretend I didn't miss her. Didn't need her. Pretend I didn't want her to come back, stay, and protect me.

Then I heard it.

Voices.

Doors opening.

"What's going on out here?"

"Them girls fighting?"

"That ain't—is that Pearl's grandbabies?"

Neighbors. Coming out onto their porches. Standing at their screen doors. Watching.

Mr. Henderson from two houses down. Miss Rita with her hair still in rollers. Some kids I recognized from school. All of them stared. Some shaking their heads. Some entertained, like this was better than whatever was on TV.

The audience.

God created the audience to push me into obedience.

Embarrassment flooded me—hot and thick like the summer air. My face burned. My throat tightened.

I stopped struggling.

Sheritta must've felt it—the fight leaving my body. She loosened her grip but didn't let go right away. Her breathing was heavy. Mine too.

"You done?" she asked quietly. Not mean. Just tired.

I nodded. Couldn't meet her eyes. Couldn't meet anyone's eyes.

She let go.

I stood there, arms hanging at my sides, feeling every pair of eyes on the block bored into me. Hoochy, the baldheaded sister. Hoochy, the troublemaker. Hoochy, fighting her own blood in the middle of the street like she had no home training.

Maybe I didn't.

"Get in the car," Sheritta said. Still quiet. Still tired.

I didn't argue this time.

I climbed back into the backseat. Nickie turned around to look at me, her expression unreadable. Concern mixed with frustration mixed with something else— maybe understanding.

Sheritta got back in the driver's seat. Started the engine. The air conditioning blasted, making me shiver despite the heat still clinging to my skin.

We pulled away from 558 Wilkins, past the watching neighbors already deciding which version of this story they'd tell. Past the house where Grandma was probably passed out by now, the iron still lying on the floor where it fell.

Nobody spoke.

I stared out the window, jaw clenched, eyes burning but refusing to cry. I wasn't hurt. I wasn't scared.

I was embarrassed. And mad.

Mad at Sheritta for leaving. Mad at God for using shame as a leash. Mad at the neighbors for watching. Mad at myself for caring what any of them thought.

But most of all, I was mad because somewhere underneath all that anger, I knew the truth:

I needed her. I needed all of them.

And needing people had never gotten me anything but left behind.

I always thought "Curb Ball" was just a simple street game. But now, after everything—the lies, the fear, the surprise tucked inside George's story—I see why they call it a curveball. Like that pitch in baseball, it's meant to throw you off, make you doubt what you think you know. I believed George killed Mom, only to learn he went to jail for something else entirely—something closer to home, but not what I expected. Life throws wild pitches you never saw coming, and you either catch them or get hit.

And just like that game, the rules aren't always clear, and the stakes aren't points on a playground—they're real.

Now Nickie's stepping into her own game, one with rules she never asked for, where the adults aren't always watching, and protection becomes something you either learn or lose.

Nobody told me this was what little girls were supposed to learn. Nobody said, "Hoochy, here's how you protect yourself when the adults can't." But I learned anyway. Because I had to.

December Days.

My first honest prayer didn't sound like church. It sounded like breath fogging the window and the radiator ticking its old song.

I lay there in the blue light of snow and said, "God... if You're there, I'm here. That's all I got." No promises. No deals. Just a soft hello after years of not speaking.

Nothing split the ceiling. No angel. No warm rush. Just a quiet that didn't feel empty anymore.

Small things started holding me without grabbing: the bus driver who waited an extra two seconds while I ran; Miss Parker pressing a second cocoa in my hands and saying, "Stay warm, baby"; Grandma humming a hymn over folded towels, and somehow her voice carried a prayer for me.

Nickie tossed me the better mitten without making a big deal of it. The streetlight outside kept steady for once, no buzzing, no flicker. A dime in my coat pocket on the day we needed bus fare. Church bells three blocks away sounded like spoons tapping glass, bright and thin and enough.

I stopped asking for big signs and started noticing small mercies—the way snow hushed the block, how the sun laced our alley in glitter, the ache in my chest easing for half a minute at a time.

My prayers stayed short and honest: Please. Thank You. I'm scared. I'm here. And, little by little, that felt safe enough to say.

December was another favorite time of year for us—not for Christmas or school break, but for the snow I loved. Snowmen and fortresses rose right outside our front window.

Before the climate and ozone issues, it really used to snow 10 to 12 inches in most Decembers, sometimes in a single day. School was out only after seven inches were announced on the news.

We'd wake to the TV downstairs while my grandmother waited until the last minute to deliver her usual morning alarm: "Y'all going to school today?"

Of course, my under-my-breath answer never changed: "No." But I'd get up anyway.

On snowy nights, I'd stay up, looking out the rusty-framed bedroom window, tracking how much had fallen. Across the street, a fire hydrant sat on the corner, and if the snow reached the first line before the opening where the hose went, I knew we had about six or seven inches—and no school.

In the morning, the newscaster would finally say the magic words: "All Detroit Public Schools are closed today."

That's all I needed to hear.

Believe it or not, I'd be up and dressed faster on a Snow Day than on any regular school morning. As the snow kept falling, I'd throw on whatever I could grab—mismatched, layered, barely zipped—and head for the door.

Downstairs, I already heard the chaos: stomping boots, pacing footsteps, doors slamming, siblings arguing. I stayed out of it. Whatever they were mad about didn't involve me—not today.

Outside was calling.

The cold Michigan morning started with heavy grey-blue skies, the sun barely punching through thick snow clouds. In just a few hours, it would be dark again—and with it, the fun would fade.

My grandmother did the best she could to provide for us. We had proper winter clothes, but, like most kids, we didn't keep them in good condition. I had boots, a coat, a hat—never mine, always borrowed—and socks for gloves.

We'd rub Vaseline on our hands before pulling on the socks to keep out the cold. The more socks, the better, especially if we wanted to stay out long enough to build our snow fortress.

We used my grandmother's old red Thanksgiving chitlin bucket, the one she also used for mopping. The bucket was perfectly rectangular, and when we packed it with snow and flipped it over, it looked like the start of an igloo.

Then came the snowball fights, snow angels, and throwing snowballs at passing cars.

"Hoochy, don't throw that snowball at those cars—you're gonna get in trouble!" Nickie said, shaking her head. "I'm not doing it."

I smirked. "You're such a scardy cat."

Yes, I know it's "scaredy cat." In my Midwest Michigan dialect, we say it our own way—like how we say stow instead of store, or melk instead of milk.

A Cadillac Outside, No Santa Inside

It was the winter of 1981, one of those real Michigan winters that seemed to last forever. The temperature was in the mid-20s to low-30s, with about ten to fifteen inches of snow. School was closed, and Nickie and I were outside making dirty snowmen—the kind that turned brown from rolling across the street and picking up dirt.

I started throwing snowballs at cars again, and Nickie gave me the same speech: "Don't do it."

But I, with my bottom lip poked out and head bobbing with pride—or maybe mischief—ignored her. That was my mistake.

With that much snow and unplowed streets, cars crawled through the neighborhood. You just hoped the sun melted the snow before the plows came.

I wound up, my right arm ready, and launched a snowball—probably a good 35 miles per hour.

Splat! Direct hit. Driver's side window. Black Cadillac.

The car stopped. The driver jumped out. "Come here, you b****! You hit my car!"

I froze, not from the cold, but from fear. My body didn't move until my brain screamed, Run!

I bolted straight through the front door and up the stairs to my room.

Then came the pounding on the door—more like banging. "Open up! That little b**** hit my car with a snowball!"

I heard muffled voices—my grandmother, the man, and my uncle—arguing. Then a door shut. Heavy footsteps stomped up the stairs.

I slid under my brother's bed, between the crates holding up his mattress and box spring.

"Hoochy, where are you?" my uncle shouted.

I thought, Oh, I'm good. He's not going to do anything to me. I started crawling out—then a hand grabbed my arm and yanked me hard. The bed collapsed as he pulled, the crates crashing down on my feet.

"I'm tired of you guys!" he yelled, his face inches from mine. "Ever since y'all came to live with us, my mother's had to give you bad-ass kids all her attention and no time for me!"

"Let me go! You better not touch me—I'll tell Grandma!" I shouted, snatching my shirt from his grip.

"I hate y'all! I wish you had died instead of my sister!"

"GRANDMA!" I screamed, flying down the stairs so fast my feet barely touched them. I gripped the banister like a gymnast between swings, launching from one section to the next, until I landed hard at the bottom and darted toward the kitchen, where Grandma always was.

"Grandma! Uncle said he wished I had died with my mom!"

She yelled his name, telling him to come downstairs. No response. He had already climbed out the window onto the tin roof and left the house.

My behavior didn't come from anger—it came from hurt. Pain, for me, was how I fought, how I found strategy in the chaos—a call for help. A motion. An action. A voice for what I couldn't explain—the misery, the feeling of being unwanted.

December was my favorite month growing up because of the snow. For most kids, Christmas was the reason—Santa, gifts, and magic. But I realized early there was no Santa in the Projects.

Every story said Santa came down the chimney, and we didn't have one. Our heat came from old cast-iron radiator boilers that pushed hot water through metal units that hissed with steam.

We loved those radiators, especially in winter. The moment we came inside from the cold, we'd rush to them, hanging our wet clothes and socks to dry. Because of that heat—and maybe the humidity—I don't remember us getting sick much.

Sometimes, when we had candy—especially Now-N-Laters—we'd unwrap them, set them on paper, and place them on the radiator to melt. They'd get soft and stretchy, the perfect kind of chewy. You'd burn your tongue trying to eat them before they hardened again, but it was worth it.

As for Christmas, it wasn't anything special. Thanksgiving was the real holiday in our house.

Christmas meant Goodfellow gift boxes, maybe a card from my grandfather and grandmother—Jerry's dad and stepmother—who would send a hundred-dollar check for Grandma to buy us gifts. Sometimes I could tell when that money was spent on us because those gifts were the ones hidden deep in the "secret closet."

That closet sat halfway between the front room and Grandma's favorite place, the kitchen. Old coats and clothes hung in front, blocking the back like a tunnel. To us kids, it was a world of mystery, a hiding place, and, during December, a treasure cave.

Many days, we'd send Nickie in there to "check for gifts." I'd whisper, "Hey, Nickie, Grandma said we could open one present early."

"Really?" she'd say, eyes wide. "Stop playing—she didn't say that."

"She did," I'd lie. "But since Fat-al and I got in trouble, you're the only one who gets to open one early. Come on, let's go look."

She'd hesitate, but her hope always gave her away. Nickie loved her siblings and wanted so badly to be included—to be loved back the same way she loved us. She resembled our mother more than any of us, and people commented on her beauty all the time. I don't think she wanted that attention—she wanted to be seen.

Nickie slept with her eyes halfway open—always had, even as a little girl. Back then, I thought it was just weird. Later, I wondered if she kept her eyes open to watch me and my pranks... or to keep watch over herself.

When we pulled that closet prank, we always made sure Grandma was asleep on the couch. We knew if she didn't move when we walked by, she was sleeping hard, maybe from being tired—raising four kids plus her own, past fifty-five—or maybe from "the consumption," as I called it, because of the faint smell that lingered from the kitchen to her couch.

"Go ahead, Nickie," I'd say, pushing her toward the closet. "Grandma said it's okay—before she went to sleep."

Fat-al would be right behind me, sometimes our cousin, too, all of us giggling. Nickie would push past the coats, saying, "It's dark—I can't see anything!"

That's when we'd push her in, shut the door, and yell, "Grandma! Nickie's trying to see the Christmas gifts early!"

Then we'd run upstairs laughing while Grandma's voice roared through the house.

Those were fun times—at least, that's what I told myself.

At Christmas, Grandma always placed oranges and pecans on the table. We loved it—it was a snack for us.

Of course, there were also those Goodfellow candies— multi-colored, glossy, and clumped together from sitting in the bowl too long—and the old peppermints that never quite dissolved in your mouth.

When we returned to school after the break, all the kids bragged about their Christmas gifts and new clothes. There I was, sitting in my Goodfellow jeans—you could always tell. They were the darkest blue, with thick stitches and stiff fabric that could stand on their own. No brand tags, no name stitched on the pocket—just plain.

Embarrassed, I'd stay quiet.

The kids already knew who got Goodfellow boxes because, before break, the school would call your name over the PA: "Yolanda Washington, please come to the library to get your Goodfellow box."

I'd stand up slowly, trying not to look at anyone, hoping someone else's name would be called right after mine. I'd walk out pretending it didn't matter, but inside, I felt the sting of shame.

All that for a box with socks, jeans, a shirt, candy, and a bald-headed doll.

At church, we'd do speeches again and hear about the birth of Jesus and the Star that led the wise men. I used to wonder—was that the same star I climbed out the window to talk to, sitting on the tin roof in the cold night air?

I'd look up and whisper, "Why me?" Why did Jesus' birth mean so much to people when mine brought my mother pain?

God, why am I here? And if You love me, why did You take my parents from me? I'm sorry. Please give them back.

That same star I cried to in those December nights seemed to whisper back through the wind: "I'm here, and I love you."

I didn't understand it then, but years later—after anger had loosened its grip—I recognized that voice. It was the same still, quiet voice that had been with me all along.

Even in that house where I looked out during those cold December days, where snow fell heavily and I found laughter to cover pain like frost on glass—God was there.

Strategy Was My Superpower
AGES 11–12 — LEARNING TO OUTSMART THE WORLD THAT TRIED TO BREAK ME

One thing I learned: Shanky's kids had a certain charm— a knack for manipulating, attracting, and befriending men just enough that those men would protect them.

At ten, I started to see my own "Shanky Power." It didn't come from attraction—Nickie and Sheritta had that. It wasn't from befriending either; that was Fat-al.

Mine was a strategy.

Not manipulation, as I saw it—more like DNA crossed with investigation—building a plan around their likes, dislikes, their angles.

Before then, even as a tomboy, I had female friends at school. But boys still came to me because I was often around my brother and uncle.

They'd sit with me; I'd ask one question, and before they knew it, they were talking longer than they'd planned.

It started small. A question about basketball. A comment on new sneakers. An observation that made them feel seen, even when I was the one nobody wanted to look at.

I watched them respond—watched shoulders drop, voices ease. Watched them forget, for a moment, that I was supposed to be invisible.

I was learning a language that had nothing to do with my face or my body. The language of attention. Of listening. Of making someone feel like they mattered.

And once I learned it, I realized: this was power.

One day, at St. Peter Claver Activity Center—the neighborhood spot that felt nothing like the Brewster Center—I felt that power sharpen.

St. Peter actually had employees you could talk to about after-school goals, arts, and talent. It was real outreach—a neighborhood center.

Brewster Center felt like a barn stocked with hay and water, where we—like cattle—were herded together. It kept us contained with swimming, basketball, softball, and free lunches, but there were hardly any people around except the cleaning staff. We never saw the farmer—only the product we were fed.

Later, I understood we were the ones being prepared for slaughter—boys and girls alike. The farmers only surfaced to claim what they wanted from the product.

Some of us got taken early. Some of us learned to hide. Some of us never made it out. We'll explore that truth later.

Back to St. Peter.

The building was a red-brick hub for community, recreation, and social services, especially for youth and families from the predominantly African American housing development. The center had multi-purpose rooms for basketball, swimming, and educational support, mirroring the amenities at the nearby Brewster-Wheeler Recreation Center—gymnasiums, classrooms, and event halls.

St. Peter Claver sat at 450 Eliot Street.

Each time I went to St. Peter, nostalgia hit—a pang for Eliot, for what I could barely remember. I'd look down the street and say to myself, I live down there. Or I used to. The address was still in me, even if the home wasn't.

St. Peter had a gym where men lifted weights, and I followed my uncle there. I loved the place; it was a way to get away from home.

The weight room was in the basement, down a flight of concrete stairs that echoed with every step. The walls were painted that industrial yellow-beige all old buildings wore—chipped in places, water-stained in others. The air smelled like rust, sweat, and the faint tang of old rubber mats that had absorbed years of dropped weights and heavy breathing.

A single row of fluorescent lights buzzed overhead, casting a harsh, flat glow. In one corner sat a bench press with mismatched plates—some black iron, some gray, concrete-filled. A pull-up bar hung from exposed pipes. Free weights lined a crooked rack against the wall, dumbbells from five to fifty pounds, some with duct tape holding the plates together.

It wasn't fancy. But to the men who came there, it was sacred.

"Hey, Hoochy," the guys would say when I came in.

They knew me. And they knew my uncle and his pull in the community. Their faces tilted up when they said hello, like their stomachs were upset. I knew that look— I'd seen it too many times before turning 11, the distorted face of disgust at my looks.

The slight curl of the upper lip. The quick flick of the eyes away, then back, then away again. The forced smile that never reached the eyes. The way their bodies pulled back just a fraction, like I was something unpleasant to endure.

That was fine. I didn't want them looking at me the way my other "uncles" looked at Nickie.

I'd seen those looks too—the ones that lingered too long, traveled up and down, made my sister shrink into herself even as she smiled. The ones that made my stomach turn and my fists clenched. The ones that meant danger in a different language.

So let them be disgusted. Let them look away. That was safer.

"Hey, Dubble," I said once. "I saw you lift all that weight—how much was it?"

Dubble was one of the regulars—mid-twenties, dark-skinned, built like he'd been lifting since he was a kid. He wore a faded gray tank with "Detroit" across the chest, the letters cracked and peeling. His arms were thick, veins running like rivers under his skin. Sweat beaded on his forehead and slipped down his temples.

I didn't quite meet his eyes. My gaze hovered near the bench where he'd laid his towel, pacing between the bench, his chin, and the floor—as if careful not to disturb the air between us.

But the bravery came from inside.

My voice wasn't loud—never that—but it carried a hard edge, a quiet demand for respect, no matter the sneer or side-eye he threw. Inside, a stubborn little fire pushed me forward, telling me I deserved more, that beneath all the judgments there was a part of me they hadn't seen yet.

Soft, hesitant—part question, part defense—I asked, "So... how much can you all lift?"

He paused mid-wipe. Looked at me like he was deciding whether I was worth the breath.

Then he started talking.

He told the story of when he first lifted, and I sat there listening—no interruptions, full attention. My face opened; my eyes widened with each step of his journey, following with suspense and curiosity.

He talked about being a skinny kid, wanting to be strong so nobody would mess with him. About the first time he benched his body weight. About his goal to hit 300 pounds before he turned thirty.

And I listened. Really listened. Not because I cared about bench numbers, but because I cared about what it meant to him.

In seconds, his expression shifted—jaw eased, eyes softened, brow relaxed, voice calmer. Believe me, I noticed.

The disgust melted. Not completely—it never did—but enough. Enough that he saw me as a person instead of an eyesore. Enough that he kept talking.

As my voice reached outward, it still wasn't mine—it was anger, calculation, survival. My brain had been stitched from wanting love into wanting control and respect. I didn't need love. God was supposed to supply that, according to the Bible, and since He seemed to have forgotten me between Eliot and Wilkins, I decided I would love myself in a way no one could touch—physically, mentally, or with their looks.

You know the look: a restrained grimace disguised as neutral; eyebrows twitching up for an instant, registering something they wouldn't call ugly out loud but filing it quietly in the drawer for what doesn't please the eye.

I learned to see it coming. Learned to brace. Then learned to disarm it before it could wound me.

"Oh man," I would end the conversation, "you're much better at this than my uncle," with a wink.

Heading back to the weights, Dubble would find himself turning and nodding. "Hey, Hoochy," he'd say before leaving the gym—no more disgust. "You gonna be here tomorrow? I'm lifting 225."

"Sure," I'd say.

As the guys left, they waved goodbye. At first, plenty still looked and waved with disdain. But some found my attention engaging enough that they left with half-smiles, as if carrying away something they couldn't name.

I gave them what they needed: to be heard. To matter.

And in return, they gave me something too: safety. Protection. A respect that had nothing to do with my face.

It was transactional maybe. But it was survival.

St. Peter would host "Friday Disco" for the kids in the neighborhood, 25 cents to get in.

The disco was in the same basement as the weight room, but on Friday nights, it transformed. They'd push the weights aside, roll out a portable DJ booth, and string up colored lights—red, blue, green—that spun and flashed to the beat. The music hit hard enough to feel in your chest: Michael Jackson, Rick James, Prince, The Gap Band.

Kids packed in—project kids, neighborhood kids, kids from the Catholic school down the street. We danced until we were drenched, the air thick and humid, the concrete walls catching every bass drop.

For 25 cents, you could forget everything else. You could just be a kid.

Every week before Friday, Nickie and I would gather pennies and dimes to reach the quarter—even if that meant stealing from my grandmother's change cup on the table in the front room where we ate. We'd wait until she fell asleep and sneak it out, depending on how much was in the cup. If there was only a little, we knew she'd notice and we'd get in trouble, but sometimes there was more than two dollars in change. If there were quarters, we took those.

I planned it before I took it—down to telling my grandmother, "It looks like you have three dollars of change in the cup. Can I have some?" She would say no. But really it was only two dollars, so when we took some, she wouldn't notice.

Strategy—always strategy, always.

Nickie and I entered the dance contest every Friday. Whenever she showed up, she placed first—95% of the time. I came in second or third. First got a dollar; second, fifty cents.

Nickie could dance. Really dance. Not just the steps, but the feeling—the way her body moved like the music came from inside her instead of the speakers. People would form a circle around her, clapping and hyping her up. She'd smile—really smile—in a way I rarely saw at home.

One time I came in first while Nickie competed, and she turned on me like a hyena—switching packs, following the stronger group to survive. She went off with Fay and the other girls, and I walked home by myself.

I stood there holding that dollar, watching her walk away with them. Their laughter carried back to me on the night air, sharp and cutting.

She didn't look back.

I told myself I didn't care. I told myself I was used to it. But that night, the walk home felt longer.

Darkness Revealed My Light

Some places shape you quietly—where the walls seem to listen, where even the light hums a secret. For me, St. Peter Claver Activity Center was one of those places. It was where my shadows met my reflection, where I first felt the strange power of becoming.

Before I ever knew strength had a name, I learned it in silence. Like Batman watching the city from rooftops, I was learning how to survive in the dark—how to take pain and make it useful. I didn't know it then, but the darkness wasn't my enemy; it was the backdrop that made my light impossible to ignore.

One day, at St. Peter Claver Activity Center—on the way home, a man in a van slowed beside me.

The street was dark—most of the streetlights on that block were broken, shot out, or just never fixed. The ones that worked cast weak orange circles that barely touched, leaving long stretches of shadow in between.

My footsteps echoed. The disco music still thumped faintly behind me, but it was fading fast. Ahead, the street was empty. No cars. No people on porches. Just me and the sound of my own breathing.

Then I heard it: the low rumble of an engine, easing down.

My heart kicked up. I kept walking, eyes forward, but my whole body became tense.

The van pulled up beside me. White. Paneled. No windows in the back. The kind of van that made every kid in the neighborhood nervous.

"Hey, you okay? Need a ride home?"

The voice was male. Older. Trying to sound friendly, concerned. But there was something underneath—something oily and wrong.

I glanced over without turning my head. Saw him leaning across the passenger seat, window rolled down. Couldn't make out his face in the dark—just the shape of him, the gleam of his eyes.

My stomach dropped. My skin prickled. Every instinct screamed: Run.

I knew that look from Momma's friends.

"No—my uncle is right behind me, following me home," I said, stopping and turning my body in the opposite direction. I didn't run. Running meant prey. Running meant he'd chase.

"Where? I don't see him," the man said. His voice had an edge now. Testing me. Calling my bluff.

The van crept forward, keeping pace with me. I could hear the engine idling, smell the exhaust.

My mind raced. Calculated. Planned.

"Oh, he's right behind me—right by that police car on the corner. He probably got stopped by those police... because they said a man was messing with girls walking home from the disco, and they put a car out for safety. You want me to get him?"

I stopped walking. Turned toward the van. Made my voice loud and confident.

"UNCLE!" I yelled behind me. "Hey, Unk, this man in the van wants to take me home."

The van took off. Tires squealing. Gone in seconds.

I stood there, heart hammering, hands shaking. My voice had been steady, but now my legs felt like water.

That was partly true—there was an officer who sat on Mack and Eliot each night—but not my Unk. The yelling was my way of telling someone, anyone, that I was walking home scared and alone.

I looked back toward the corner where the cop car usually parked. It was there—just sitting, engine running, officers doing paperwork or eating a donut or half-asleep.

But my Unk wasn't there. He hadn't been there at all. He hadn't been home in months. Now we had to go visit him in a building with all windows and no doors.

And right then, standing alone on that empty street with my heart still trying to punch through my ribs, I felt it all crash down on me.

The anger.

Not at the van. Not at the predator who'd circled me like I was nothing. That was just the world showing me what it thought I was worth.

No—I was furious at them. At all of them.

At Unk for leaving me. For making choices that took him away instead of keeping him behind me on nights like this.

At Momma for not seeing—not noticing the looks, the hands, the weight of grown men's eyes on a child's body.

At God. For making me a girl in a world that saw girls as prey.

But most of all—most of all—I was angry at myself. For having to be this smart. This fast. This aware. For knowing that my survival depended on playing chess with predators while other kids got to just be kids.

I was tired of saving myself.

But I had me. Only me.

And I'd have to be enough.

I walked the rest of the way home fast, checking over my shoulder every few steps. That night I walked home angry, learning the first lesson of survival: Nobody's coming. Save yourself.

That's what I call Shanky's Power. In fear, my strategic mind kicked in—defending myself the way I saw Shanky defend herself when I was a kid. I used to think she just fell near that chair during the fight. But I know now the fall was deliberate. She was positioning herself to grab the knife.

Strategy wasn't just about getting what you wanted. It was about staying alive.

That night with the van, I'd done the same thing. Calculated. Lied. Positioned myself. Made him think consequences were waiting in the dark.

Like Batman, the trauma of losing his parents turned him into a villain disguised as a hero.

It didn't take me long to understand my power after that. Or was it really power? Or just survival dressed up as a game I had to play?

Strategy or Is It Manipulation?

The times I tricked Nickie into doing something by playing on her kindness remind me of when my grandmother put me on punishment and told me I couldn't go outside. I'd walk into the kitchen and stand next to her, folding my arms the way she did, copying her every move just to get under her skin.

"Girl, get away from me and go somewhere," she'd finally snap.

"I can't," I'd say. "I'm on punishment, remember?"

I'd shadow her, in and out of the kitchen, until she finally threw up her hands and said, "Then go outside and get away from me."

Got her.

I carried that same behavior through every grade with Ms. King—and later, into fifth grade, at 11 years old, with my new teacher, Mr. Mitchell.

When I realized my fifth-grade teacher was a man, I thought, this is going to be easy. All I had to do was cry— just a little, soft and sad, the kind that makes people feel sorry for you. Fake crying about not having parents always worked before.

With Mr. Mitchell, I'd greet him sweetly every morning, my voice polite, calm, respectful.

"Good morning, Mr. Mitchell. How's your day going?"

He ate it up every time.

"Heads-up, Yolanda," he'd say with a smile. "We're having a pop quiz on yesterday's math."

Trying to get out of it, I'd put my hand over my stomach and slow my walk to my seat.

"What's wrong?" he asked.

"Nothing," my face said, though my steps told on me. "My stomach is upset."

I kept that act going for weeks, maybe months—until one day the pain was real.

Everything & Everyone Leaves
AGE 12 — THE SLOW GOODBYE TO CHILDHOOD

It was true—my stomach really did hurt. The pain started low, under my belly, coming and going at first, then settling into a grinding, cramping ache that bent me over. It felt yucky, like something was wrong in my private place.

I remember in the Fifth grade. Sitting in Mr. Mitchell's class, trying to focus on fractions, and all I could think about was the throbbing in my lower abdomen and the weird, wet feeling between my legs.

Something was wrong. Really wrong.

"Mr. Mitchell, can I go to the bathroom?" I asked.

"Go ahead," he said, barely looking up from his desk.

I stood slowly, carefully, holding my stomach. A few kids glanced at me, but most kept working, passing notes, or staring out the window.

I headed for the second-floor restroom, the closest one. A few girls were inside, laughing, so I slipped away and decided to go downstairs.

The hallway was empty. Quiet, except for the muffled sounds of teachers' voices behind closed doors. My footsteps echoed on the linoleum. Each step sent a new wave of cramping through my belly.

Mrs. Stars, the school counselor, saw me bent over, heard me, and walked up to ask what was wrong.

Mrs. Stars was a Black woman in her fifties, always dressed nice—skirts and blouses, hair pressed and curled, glasses on a chain around her neck. She smelled like cocoa butter and peppermint. Her voice was gentle but firm, the kind that made you feel safe and accountable at the same time.

"I don't know. I don't feel well," I managed.

Before I could reach the stall, I threw up and collapsed.

The world tilted. My vision blurred. I felt her hands catch me before I hit the floor.

"Let me help you," Mrs. Stars said. "Hoochy"—some teachers called me that because they lived in the neighborhood and knew how much I hated Yolanda— "did you know your pants are wet in the back? Come on, let me help you."

Wet?

Inside the stall, I peeled off my pants. My underwear was wet with blood. I didn't understand, so I ran out with my pants around my knees and blurted, "I'm bleeding! Am I going to die?"

Panic flooded me. Blood meant hurt. Blood meant something was broken. Blood meant—

Mrs. Stars laughed a little, a hand over her mouth. "You got your period."

"My what?" I'd never heard of such a thing. The word—period—hit me like something foreign.

She explained it to me there in the bathroom, her voice calm and matter-of-fact. About bodies changing. About becoming a woman. About it happening every month.

Every month?

A memory flashed: before Sheritta left, I'd heard my grandmother yelling at her for starting hers. Panic rose. My grandmother is going to be mad at me, like she was at my sister.

Mrs. Stars found me a pad and clean underwear from the school's little room of necessities—toothpaste, socks, deodorant—things kids in the neighborhood sometimes couldn't afford. I'd been in that room once or twice a month for toothpaste or socks; now it was maxi pads.

She showed me how to use the pad, how to position it, how to keep myself clean. She was patient. Kind. She didn't make me feel ashamed, even though I felt it anyway—hot and heavy in my chest.

She let me go home early.

I walked the few blocks to 558 Wilkins slowly, the pad feeling thick and strange between my legs, my stomach still cramping, my mind racing with what I'd say to Grandma.

At home, I told my grandmother. Just like I'd feared, she was furious.

"Who did you sleep with?" she demanded. "You're a fast-tailed girl now."

Her face was twisted with anger and something else—fear, maybe. Or disgust. She stood over me in the kitchen, hands on her hips, beer breath sharp in my face.

"Nobody!" I said. "I didn't do nothing! Mrs. Stars said it's supposed to happen—"

"Don't lie to me, girl. You out there doing something. That's why you bleeding."

I tried to explain. Tried to tell her what Mrs. Stars said. But she wasn't listening. She never listened when her mind was already made up.

The year before, when my breasts started to grow and I asked for a bra, she scorned me. "You don't need no bra. You ain't got nothing."

So I went to school without one sometimes, wearing two shirts to hide what I had. Crossing my arms over my chest in the hallways. Hunching my shoulders forward to make myself smaller.

Once, during a fight with a girl, my shirt was torn, and my chest was exposed. The boys stared like I'd gone from tomboy to something else entirely—and the harassment began.

"Hoochy got titties!"

"Let me see, let me see!"

Hands reaching. Eyes leering. Voices that used to ignore me now followed me down the halls.

That day marked the beginning of womanhood in the neighborhood. I felt different physically, and I could feel the world looking at me with new, sharper eyes.

Eyes that used to look away in disgust now lingered. Now assessed. Now saw me as something they could take.

I hated it.

The Shift: What's Changed

I had to leave some things behind—the constant ache for my mother and father, the endless why me? I wasn't going to wait for God to hand me answers. If he'd forgotten me somewhere between Eliot and Wilkins, I would make my own way.

I decided I wouldn't let people mistreat me, look down on me, or write me off anymore. I would fight.

I wasn't a child about to bloom; I was a preteen with a hot line of anger under my skin—rebellious, ready to push back against anyone who tried me. I hadn't yet seen how much that anger fought me, too—how it chipped away at me, bit by bit. In the moment, anger felt like armor.

It felt like the only thing keeping me standing.

So once, when a boy started bullying a skinny kid for getting the answer right—taunting him loud enough for the whole class to hear—I shoved the bully out of his chair and planted my foot on his back like I was claiming victory for the different and the small.

The class erupted. Some kids laughed. Some gasped. The bully scrambled to his feet, face red, fists clenched.

"Yolanda! Principal's office. Now!"

They sent me to the office. I put on the performance— big, wet tears, the same lines I'd used before.

"I miss my mother and my dad," I said, voice cracking. "I only act out because I don't have parents."

It worked like clockwork. The principal blinked, softened, and fell for it. He'd call my grandmother, and I'd already be calculating the next move—my mind strategic even in sorrow.

"Yolanda, I'm not going to punish you this time," he'd say. "Talk to Mr. Flood, your counselor, and see if he can get your family some resources."

Then he'd hand me a pass and let me go back to class, sure he'd done the right thing.

I knew my grandmother would be lying on the couch, snoring straight through the call. I knew the routine. I knew the timing. I knew how to use other people's pity like a key.

That's how I learned to survive: not by asking for mercy, but by planning for it.

By this time, I had perfected the art of reading rooms, people, and situations. I knew who to avoid, who to charm, and who to manipulate. I knew when to cry, when to fight, when to disappear.

I knew how to make myself useful so people wouldn't throw me away.

I knew how to make myself invisible so people wouldn't see me as prey.

I knew how to turn my face—the one people grimaced at—into a weapon. If they wouldn't love me, they'd respect me. Or fear me. Or need me.

One way or another, they'd remember I existed.

The seasons kept turning. Fall gave way to winter. My twelfth birthday came and went with little fanfare—a cupcake from the corner store, maybe, if I was lucky. Mostly it was just another day.

Nickie, thirteen, was pulling further away, spending more time with boys and friends I didn't know. Fat-al was quieter than ever, retreating into books and homework and a world I couldn't reach.

Grandma's drinking got worse. The house got colder, not just from the weather but from the weight of everything unsaid.

And I got harder.

Harder in my voice. Harder in my walk. Harder in the way I looked at people who tried to hurt me.

I wasn't the little girl who played in the mud outside 657 anymore. I wasn't the five-year-old who cried when the ambulance took her mother away.

I was something else now. Something sharper. Something that had learned to cut before I got cut.

Thirteen Came for Us All

By the time I turned thirteen, the anger had settled deep into my bones like the winter cold—constant, numbing, familiar.

I'd learned to measure time in seasons—not by months or birthdays, but by what each one gave or took away.

Summer meant freedom. Winter meant watching everything die.

But thirteen was the year everything shifted. The year Nickie disappeared for good. The year I learned that danger didn't always announce itself with sirens— sometimes it just slowed down beside you in a field. The year I watched Grandma waste away while pretending she was fine. The year Fat-al started showing up, looking more and more like the ghosts I'd tried to forget.

The year I realized you can lose people in more ways than death.

During the summers, Nickie and I would head downtown for the Summer Festivals. Every weekend had a theme—the Hoe-Down, the Jazz Festival, the Luau. And every weekend, that was Nickie's world.

The festivals transformed downtown Detroit into something magical. Hart Plaza would fill with stages, food vendors, craft booths, and thousands of people— Black folks, white folks, families, couples, teenagers running wild. The air smelled of funnel cakes and barbecue smoke, beer and river water. Music poured from every direction—jazz, blues, Motown, country, depending on the weekend.

Colored lights were strung between lampposts, reflecting off the Detroit River. The Ambassador Bridge lit up in the distance, connecting us to Canada, to somewhere else, to the possibility of escape.

For a few hours, we weren't project kids. We were just kids.

Grandma had only one rule: Be on the porch when the streetlights come on.

That was it. We didn't even have to go inside—we could stay out as late as 11 p.m., as long as we were planted on that porch by the time the pole light on Wilkins flickered on, right around nine.

It was the same rule she'd had for years, the one that governed all our summers. But at thirteen, with Nickie now fourteen and pulling away, it felt different. Heavier. More like a countdown.

Me? I watched and learned.

While Nickie was busy flirting and laughing with boys— feeding off their attention, soaking up the way they said her name—I focused on the smell of funnel cakes and barbecue smoke, the shine of festive lights, and the taste of freedom that lived outside Grandma's house.

I'd wander between the booths, watching artists paint, listening to musicians tune their instruments, studying the way people moved through crowds. The way couples held hands. The way groups of teenagers traveled in packs, laughing too loud, claiming space.

I'd buy a lemonade with quarters I'd scrounged and make it last two hours, sipping slowly, savoring the cold sweetness and the fact that I'd bought it myself. That nobody had to give it to me. For a moment, I controlled something.

"Nickie, it's getting late. You know we gotta be home before the streetlights come on," I'd remind her, again and again.

She'd wave me off without looking, her attention fixed on whatever boy had caught her eye that night.

By she'd changed. Missing curfews. Sneaking out. Running with boys who didn't care about porch lights or rules. Boys who looked at her the way men looked at Momma—hungry and dangerous and promising things they'd never deliver.

Nickie had grown into her body—Momma's body, really. Slim frame and soft curves, smooth dark skin, eyes that tilted up at the corners. She'd developed that walk, too—that same walk Momma had, all twist and sway, hips moving like Marilyn Monroe. The boys couldn't look away.

And Nickie knew it. Liked it. Used it.

"Go find something to eat," she'd toss over her shoulder, swinging her hips as she walked toward a group of boys posted up near the water.

"Nickie, it's time to go! We're gonna get in trouble!"

She'd laugh—not at me, but at the idea that trouble mattered. That Grandma's rules still had weight. But those consequences were real.

Before I could finish, Nickie swung her arm at me, swatting the air. "Be quiet," she hissed. "She's probably already knocked out from her beer. We can just sneak in through the bottom window."

The boys around her laughed. One of them—Nick, they called him, tall and lean, a gold chain catching the festival lights—slid an arm around her shoulders. Possessive. Claiming.

My stomach turned. "I'm leaving," I said.

I started walking backward, still facing her, hoping she'd follow. But she didn't. The three boys around her— especially that boy Nick—had her full attention. She laughed too loudly, her eyes half-closed in that sweet but dangerous glow.

"Nickie!" I called again, taking ten more backward steps, nearly tripping over the curb as I turned toward home.

She didn't even look.

The Walk Home Alone, Again

The downtown Detroit Riverfront was about a thirty-minute walk from the Brewsters. In the shop windows along Woodward, a bright digital clock blinked 8:30.

If I walked, I'd barely make it before the lights came on. If I ran, maybe—just maybe—I'd look like the good girl, for once.

So I ran.

Past the department stores with their mannequins frozen in summer dresses. Past the churches with their stone steps and stained-glass windows gone dark for the night. Past the parks where homeless men slept on benches, their shopping carts parked beside them like loyal dogs.

Past the laughter and music from the festival, shrinking behind me with every step.

My feet hit the pavement in time with my heartbeat, as if I could outrun the night.

The streets changed as I ran. Downtown's bright lights and crowded sidewalks thinned into emptier blocks. Fewer people. More shadows. The buildings got shorter, more run-down. Graffiti scarred the walls. Broken windows gaped like missing teeth.

I knew these streets. Knew which corners to avoid. Knew where to cut through to save time. Knew the rhythm of danger the way some kids knew the rhythm of jump rope rhymes.

But when I reached the edge of that field—the one where I once ran for my life—my body went heavy, like I was wading through thick grease.

That field still lived in my bones.

Back then—maybe a year before, cutting through from my dad's house one summer—I'd taken a shortcut through the tall grass off Edmond. The weeds stood waist-high, thick and wild, reclaiming land the city had forgotten. I had to kick a path just to move forward, the dry stalks scratching my bare legs.

The field stretched wide and empty under a grey-blue sky. No houses nearby. No people. Just me and the rustling grass and the distant hum of traffic on the freeway.

Then—POW!—a sound ripped the air.

Sharp. Loud. Unmistakable.

A gunshot.

I spun around and couldn't tell if it came from behind, left, or right. The sound seemed to come from everywhere and nowhere. But I knew that sound. I'd heard it too many nights from my bedroom window— pop-pop-pop in the distance, sometimes followed by sirens, sometimes by nothing but silence.

My heart slammed against my ribs. My breath caught.

A man stood to my left. Maybe twenty feet away, maybe more. It was hard to tell in the tall grass.

Black jacket. Smile too wide. His head was small and round like the moon, teeth catching what little light there was. He looked straight at me.

Then his hand lifted, a black shape in his grip, metal glinting.

A gun.

I dropped into the grass like I'd been shot. Just fell, straight down, hands pressed between my legs, trying to hold back the pee threatening to come. My face hit the dirt. Dry earth filled my nose, my mouth. I squeezed my eyes shut, heart hammering so hard I thought he'd hear it.

I stayed there, still as dirt, still as death, for what felt like forever.

Counting seconds in my head. Listening for footsteps. For his voice. For the sound of him getting closer.

Nothing.

Just my breathing—fast, shallow, panicked and the rustle of grass in the wind.

When I finally peeked up, the field was empty.

No man. No gun. No proof he'd ever been there except the terror still flooding my veins.

I ran all the way home that day. Ran until my lungs burned and my legs shook. Ran past Big Dipper Store, past the six-story building, through the lot, up the steps, and straight into the house without looking back.

I didn't tell anyone. What would I say? That I saw a man with a gun? People got shot in the Brewsters every week. Nobody would care. Nobody would be surprised.

And part of me wondered: Did he shoot at me? Or near me? Or was he just showing me he could?

Was it a warning? A game? Or had I imagined the whole thing, my fear turning shadows into threats?

I never found out.

But I never cut through that field again.

So now, thirteen and running from the Summer Festival, that same memory grabbed at my ankles as I approached the field. I didn't slow down. Didn't cut through. I took the long way around, added five minutes to my route, and kept to the lit streets.

Past Big Dipper Store, where the drunks sat on overturned crates, falling over each other, lying and laughing over their dice games. The smell of cheap beer and cigarettes hung thick in the air. Someone's radio played Marvin Gaye.

"Pardon me," I said, slipping between them.

"Hoochy! Girl, what's wrong with you?" one slurred, his breath hot with beer, eyes unfocused. "You lookin' for your Uncle Milton?"

"No," I shot back, barely slowing.

"Well, you'd better slow down before you trip and bust your face!" another called after me, and they all erupted in laughter.

I kept running.

Past the six-story building where we'd watch the 4th of July fireworks from the roof—sneaking up there even though we weren't supposed to, lying on our backs on the hot tar paper, watching the sky explode in red and white and blue.

Where my brother used to pick up papers for his route, hauling the heavy stack up the stairs at 5 a.m., folding them while he walked, his bag getting lighter with each delivery.

Down Beaubien, through the lot, cutting behind the house. The sun was melting down, burnt orange sliding below the horizon, painting the sky in shades of fire.

The streetlights hadn't come on yet. Not quite. But I could feel them getting ready—that electric hum that meant they'd flicker on any second.

Two steps up, jump the six-foot slab—home.

Made it.

The screen door creaked open slowly, like it knew I was guilty even though I wasn't. Not this time.

I tried to slip in quietly, catch my breath, get upstairs before—

"Where's your sister?"

Grandma's voice cut through the kitchen. Sharp. Knowing.

She was standing at the stove, her back to me, but I could see the way her hand gripped the counter edge. White-knuckled. Like she needed it to stay upright.

"I don't know." I shrugged, chest heaving, sweat dripping down my back, soaking through my shirt.

Her eyes narrowed when she turned. She knew. She always knew.

But something else caught my attention. The way she moved—slower than usual, like each step cost her something. The way her housecoat hung loose on her frame, showing bones where there used to be flesh.

I'd been noticing it all summer. The weight dropping off her. Cancer. I didn't know the word yet, but I knew something was eating her from the inside out.

I headed upstairs, changed clothes, lay down on the bed, staring at the ceiling, waiting.

The streetlights came on. That orange glow seeped through the curtains, painting the room in amber.

Nickie wasn't home.

I waited, listening. Listening for the screen door. For her footsteps. For Grandma's voice to rise like thunder.

Nothing.

An hour passed. Maybe more.

Then—click. Ting. Click.

Something tapped against my window.

I sat up fast, peeking through the curtain. Nickie. Her face half-lit by the streetlight, hair messy, lip gloss smeared. She looked up at me, whispering, "Open the window!"

The same window we used to sneak in was our emergency entrance, the little window in the room by the stairs, the one with the old brass handle that never quite latched right. Usually, one of us would tiptoe down, twist it open, and run back up before Grandma's hearing caught the creak.

But not tonight.

I waved my hands through the glass, mouthing, I can't.

Grandma must've learned our trick. Maybe she'd locked it on purpose, waiting to see who'd try.

Nickie's eyes dropped from me to the front door.

It had opened.

Grandma stood there in her nightgown—one hand gripping the screen door, the other stretched across the frame, palm flat against the wall like a guardrail. If you wanted in, you'd have to duck under that arm and brace for what came next.

She didn't say a word. Just stood there. Waiting.

Even in the dim porch light, I could see how thin she'd gotten. How her nightgown hung like a sheet on a scarecrow. How her face looked hollow, eyes sunken deep.

Nickie froze halfway up the porch steps. "Grandma..." she whispered, voice trembling. "I-I'm sorry."

Grandma didn't move. Didn't blink. Just squinted through the darkness, lips pressed tight.

The silence stretched. The whole block seemed to hold its breath.

Finally, Grandma spoke. Her voice was low, controlled, more dangerous than yelling.

"Get your butt upstairs. And don't let me catch you outside or downtown again for a long while," she said.

Nickie ducked her head, slipped past Grandma's arm like a soldier walking into punishment, and climbed the stairs without another word.

The screen door closed with a long, slow creek. Then the heavy inside door. Then silence.

I lay back in bed, heart still racing—not from fear, but from knowing Grandma always knew. Always.

And from seeing how much it cost her to stand in that doorway. How her hand had trembled on the frame. How she'd leaned against the wall as she'd fall without it.

Nickie wanted out of 558 Wilkins. She wanted out of the projects, out of that house, that life. And nothing Grandma did could stop her.

I knew it. Grandma knew it. Nickie knew it.

It was only a matter of time.

Nickie started coming home differently.

She'd been pulling away for months—staying out later, lying about where she'd been, spending more time with boys we didn't know.

But after the festivals started, something shifted.

She'd come home with bruises she tried to hide. Long sleeves in summer heat. Turning her face away when you try to look at her too closely. Flinching when you touched her arm.

"Nickie, what happened?" I asked once, seeing the purple-yellow mark on her wrist.

"Nothing. Bumped into something."

But I knew. On some level, I knew.

The boyfriend—Benny, with his gold chain and cold eyes—had started showing up more. Waiting for her on the corner. Walking her home with his arm too tight around her shoulders. Pulling her into alleys while his friends watched and laughed.

I saw him grab her once. Saw his hand close around her throat. Saw her go still, hands hanging at her sides, not fighting.

When she came back inside, I said, "Why don't you just stop seeing him?"

She looked at me like I'd said the dumbest thing in the world. "You don't understand nothing, Hoochy."

And she was right. I didn't. Not then.

I didn't understand why she kept going back. Why didn't she tell Grandma? Why did she let him treat her that way?

But I understand now.

When you're fourteen and desperate to be loved, when every adult in your life has failed you or left you or hurt you, when you look like your mother who died choosing drugs over her own children, you start to believe that pain is just what love costs.

Those bruises are the price you pay for being wanted.

That your body isn't yours—it's just something men take, and you should be grateful they want it at all.

Benny took more than Nickie's body that summer. He took her light. Her laugh. Her hope.

And I watched it happen. Watched her disappear into something dark and dangerous. Watched her become a ghost in her own skin.

And I didn't stop it. Didn't tell anyone. Didn't save her.

Because I was thirteen and didn't know how. Because I was scared. Because I'd learned early that minding your business kept you safe.

So, I kept my mouth shut. And Nickie kept suffering.

Until one night, she came home barely able to walk. Until the bruises were too dark to hide. Until Grandma—dying herself, drinking herself numb, barely holding on— finally saw what was happening.

In our family, thirteen wasn't just an age, it was a threshold. A warning. A pattern we didn't talk about but always felt coming.
 Sheritta moved at thirteen.
 Fat-al ran away at thirteen.
Nickie slipped away at thirteen, close enough for the curse to still claim her.

And now it was my turn to face it—
 the year that came for all of us.

Three is Now Two

Then Nickie left for Job Corps at fourteen. She didn't say goodbye. Not really. One day she was there—sleeping with her eyes half-open—the next day her bed was empty. Stripped. The mattress bare—its stains showing through.

Grandma told me that morning, casually, as if it were nothing. "Your sister went to Job Corps. Get some training. Make something of herself."

I stood there in the kitchen, cereal turning to mush in my bowl, trying to process what that meant.

Job Corps. Grand Rapids, Michigan. A few hours away—might as well have been another country. A program for teenagers who needed to get away, learn a trade, and finish school somewhere that wasn't here.

It was supposed to be a good thing. An opportunity. A chance.

But all I heard was, "She left."

Left me. Left this house. Left the Brewsters. Left the only family she had.

"When's she coming back?" I asked.

Grandma shrugged, lighting a cigarette with shaking hands. "When she's done, I guess."

No details. No timeline. No promises.

Just gone.

But I knew why she left. I'd known for months, even though nobody said it out loud. Even though we all pretended everything was fine when it wasn't.

Grandma finally stepped in when Nickie came home one night, barely able to walk, when the bruises were too dark to hide. When even Grandma's beer-blurred, cancer-fogged eyes couldn't ignore what was happening.

There was yelling. Door's slamming. Grandma on the phone with someone—Auntie, maybe, or social services; I never knew who. Her voice hoarse, coughing between words—still fighting.

And then, within days, Nickie was gone.

Grand Rapids. Somewhere far enough that Nick couldn't follow. Somewhere that promised training and education and a future that wasn't the Brewsters.

But really, it was an escape. It was survival. It was get out before you ended up like your mother—dead at twenty-three with nothing to show for it but three kids who didn't understand why you left.

So, Nickie left. At fourteen. Beaten. Used. Broken in ways I couldn't see but felt like a shadow following her through the house.

She needed to go. Needed to get away from this place, from Nick, from the memories of what had been done to her.

And I didn't blame her. How could I?

But that didn't make it hurt less when I woke up to her empty bed.

Loneliness

The house felt different without her. Quieter in some ways, louder in others. Her absence took up more space than her presence ever did.

I'd walk past her empty bed and feel the ache in my chest—that hollow, burning feeling that sits under your ribs and won't let you breathe right. Heartache, I guess they call it. But it felt more like heart-empty. Like something had been scooped out and nothing rushed in to fill the gap.

At night, I'd lie there staring at the ceiling, listening to the sounds of the house. Grandma coughing on the couch downstairs—deep, rattling coughs that went on and on. The radiator hissing. Sirens in the distance. The wind rattles the window frame.

And nothing else.

No Nickie breathing across the room. No whispered conversations after lights-out. No giggling over stupid pranks or shared secrets.

Just me.

Alone.

I'd tricked her. Teased her. Pushed her into closets and blamed her for things she didn't do. Used her kindness like a tool. Made her the punchline of jokes that probably hurt more than I knew.

And I hadn't protected her. Hadn't stopped Nick. Hadn't even tried.

I watched her slip away into something dark and dangerous, and I told myself it wasn't my business that she was older. That she knew what she was doing.

But she didn't. She was just a kid. Just like me. Just trying to find love in a place where love looked like violence, felt like possession, and ended up in bruises you had to hide.

And now she was gone.

Not dead like Momma. But gone in a way that felt just as permanent. Gone because staying meant dying maybe not physically, but in every other way that mattered.

She chose to leave.

She chose herself.

She chose survival over staying.

And I was left behind. Again.

The beer drinking got worse. Not just at night anymore, but during the day. By noon, she'd have that mayonnaise jar filled, drinking it slow and steady like medicine.

Maybe it was medicine, the only thing that dulled whatever pain was eating her from the inside.

She got meaner, too. Quicker to anger. Throwing things. Yelling at us for nothing. Then crying. Then apologizing. Then, forgetting she'd apologized, she'd get mad all over again.

It was like watching someone drown in slow motion. Watching them fight and tire and fight and tire until you wondered when they'd just let go and sink.

But Pearl didn't let go. Not yet.

She kept cooking—even when it hurt to stand that long. Kept cleaning—even when lifting the mop made her wince. Kept getting us ready for church even when she couldn't go herself anymore.

Kept raising us. Kept holding on. Kept standing in doorways at midnight waiting for granddaughters who came home too late, because that's what she'd always done, and she didn't know how to stop.

That year, at thirteen, I didn't understand it. Didn't understand why she kept fighting when her body was clearly giving up. But now I do.

She was all we had. And she knew it. So she'd hold on as long as she could—through cancer, through pain, through exhaustion that went bone-deep—because letting go meant leaving us behind.

And Pearl had already lost too many people she loved. She wasn't ready to add herself to that list. Not yet.

And then Fat-al started showing up. Fat-al lived in his own world, quiet, distant, barely there even when he was in the same room. We didn't talk much, but I knew something was wrong.

He wasn't living with us—he'd been gone for a while by then, bouncing between cousins and aunties and whoever would take him in for a few weeks before he wore out his welcome.

But he'd come by. Knock on the door. Stand there looking thin and hollow, eyes too bright, skin ashy and dry.

"Hey, Grandma. Can I get something to eat?"

And Grandma—dying, exhausted, barely able to stand— would let him in. Would fry him some eggs or heat up some leftovers. Would watch him eat like he hadn't seen food in days.

Because he probably hadn't.

I'd watch him from the doorway. Watch the way his hands shook when he lifted the fork. Watch the way he'd glance toward the door like he was planning his escape before he'd even finished eating.

He looked like Momma. More and more each time I saw him.

The same hollow cheeks. The same sunken eyes. The same restless energy that made you feel like, even when he was sitting still, he was running.

The same sickness.

"Fat-al, you okay?" I asked once.

He looked at me like I'd asked the dumbest question in the world. "Yeah, Hoochy. I'm good."

But he wasn't. We both knew it.

He was using. Had been for a while, probably. Following in Momma's footsteps like it was genetic. Like addiction was something you inherited along with your face and your walk and your name.

Grandma knew it too. I could see it in the way she looked at him—with pity and anger and grief all mixed together like she was watching her daughter die all over again, only this time in the body of her grandson.

"Boy, when you gonna get yourself together?" she'd say, voice sharp but eyes wet.

"I'm trying, Grandma," he'd say. And maybe he was. Maybe he meant it.

But trying didn't mean succeeding. And every time he left, I wondered if that would be the last time we'd see him.

If we'd get another call—another ambulance. Another body carried out on a stretcher while we stood watching, helpless again.

History repeating itself. The same story, different bodies. The same ending.

The loneliness settled in like winter cold—sharp at first, then numbing. You get used to it. Learn to move through it. I tried not to feel it so much.

But it never really went away.

Now, it was just me and Grandma. And Fat-al disappeared into the same streets that took Momma.

Nickie gone to Grand Rapids, trying to survive. And me. Thirteen. Watching it all fall apart.

Watching everyone leave.

Why does everyone go away?

Why am I the one who is always left behind?

What's wrong with me that nobody stays?

Why didn't You protect her?

Why didn't You protect any of us?

I'd ask these questions to the ceiling. To the stars when I climbed out on the tin roof. To God, if He was listening, which I doubted.

And no one answered.

At thirteen, I learned what it meant to be truly alone. Not just physically—though the empty bed across from mine was a constant reminder. But alone in a way that makes you realize: You are the only one who's going to save you. The only one who's going to fight for you. The only one who's going to stay.

Because everyone else? They're just passing through.

Nickie ran to survive. Grandma was sick whether she wanted to tell me or not. Fat-al was following Momma into the grave one hit at a time.

And you can't hold on tight enough to make them stay. You can't love them enough or need them enough or be good enough to keep them from leaving when survival means running—or when death means no choice at all.

Have You Ever

Have you ever had a memory so sharp it cuts straight through time?

That's what thirteen feels like to me now.

Not a whole year, but fragments: Summer festivals and Nickie's trauma away from me. A man in a field with a gun. Running home in the dark. Grandma's hand was trembling on the doorframe, her body wasting away while she still tried to raise us. Nickie's empty bed. Fat-al standing in the kitchen, looking more like a ghost. The sound of Grandma coughing blood into tissues she tried to hide.

And underneath it all, the constant hum of knowing: Nothing lasts. Not summer freedom. Not the people you love.

They all leave eventually. Or you do.

That's what thirteen taught me. That's what Nickie leaving, Grandma sick, and Fat-al disappearing taught me.

How to be alone. How to live with heartache. How to keep going when the people you love most either walk away or get taken, and either way, you're left standing, wondering if any of it ever mattered at all.

And I did keep going.

Because what else was there to do?

I stopped praying for a while, because praying to God felt like leaving a voicemail that no one ever checked.

Maybe God only listens to people who already have something worth keeping.

I Can't Became; I Can
AGE13-14 — THE SEASON THAT CAME FOR ALL OF US

By eighth grade, at Spain Middle School, "Hoochy" was famous.

At home, it was just Grandma and me. Nickie had gone off to Job Corps, Fat-al had been gone a while, and Unk had moved out on his own, which left the two of us—me and Grandma.

A bad reputation was better than none—at least that's what I thought back then. My name echoed through the PA several times a week—for skipping class, for something slick, for tagging the bathroom walls with "Hoochy" like a fool.

The teachers always knew it was me, which meant long after-school clean-up sessions with a rag and a bucket.

Up to then, I'd carried a steady C average—just enough to pass, just enough to keep Grandma from fussing too much.

"Yolanda, please come down to Mr. Flood's office," the PA speaker crackled and popped.

Mr. Pahl, my homeroom teacher—a tall white man with bowlegs and a white Lamont Sanford mustache stretched across his lip—looked down at me. His golden-brown hair had streaks of dirty blond that caught the light when he dipped his head.

"Yolanda, go ahead—and go straight to his office. YOLANDA!" he repeated, leaning in so I knew he meant it.

I saw that look several times a week—for being late, for getting sent to the principal's office, or just for wandering the halls when I should've been in class.

"Oh! Hoochy's in trouble!" the kids teased as I got up and headed out of the second-floor classroom.

Mr. Flood's office was in the old part of the building, the basement. Spain used to be Lincoln Junior High, the same school my mother attended before dropping out after eighth grade. Some of the old teachers—Mr. Kidd and Mrs. Starr—had known my mom, my siblings, and now me, the youngest.

And like I always said: I am not my siblings.

"Yolanda! Where are you going?" someone would call out in the hallway. I flashed my hall pass with pride, strutting like I owned the place. For once, I was legit.

"Hey, Mr. Flood," I said, flopping into one of the two chairs at his desk. "What's up?" I didn't make full eye contact; my hands wandered across his desk, touching papers and pens—keeping it in my comfort zone.

"Yolanda," he said.

"Mr. Flood, I told you to call me Hoochy! All the other teachers and counselors do."

"I'm not calling you that name, young lady," he said, his wide face turning red as he fidgeted in his chair, already frustrated.

"I want to let you know," he said carefully, "that if you don't pass this semester, you might not graduate."

"What do you mean?" I snapped, pushing the trinket I'd been fiddling with aside.

He pulled up my special education file.

"I thought you were calling me down here to take the Cass Tech test," I said. "Or maybe Renaissance."

Those were the top schools in Detroit. My best friend, Nick-Nick, had already taken the test—she was smart. Every year, her name got called at the awards assemblies.

I remembered another teacher who tried to tell me I couldn't.

In seventh grade, our library teacher, Ms. Wells, announced a Black American Writing Contest. She handed out papers to the first table—all the A-plus girls with perfect hair flips and pressed skirts. When she reached my table—me, Nick-Nick, Tammy—she skipped right over me.

"Hey! Where's mine?" I said.

She kept walking, smirking.

I pushed my chair back hard; it crashed to the floor. "Why can't I enter the contest?"

"Yolanda, sit down before I send you to the principal's office!"

"Send me!" I shouted. "I'm going to tell them you treat me bad—you never liked me!"

"It's 'mistreat me,' Yolanda," she snapped. "And that's exactly why you can't enter—you can't even keep up in this class!"

She kept saying "you can't" or maybe that's all I heard. Either way, it woke something in me. The spirits of Shanky, Pearl, Hoochy, and the Holy Ghost all rose at once.

"Oh yeah?" I said, snatching a copy from her hand. "I'll show you."

I filled it out right there, head down, mumbling, "No one's gonna tell me I can't."

Long story short—I came in first place. Na-na, Ms. Wells.

Back in Mr. Flood's office, he sighed. "Oh no, Hoochy—I mean, Yolanda. You can't—or won't—be considered with those math grades."

"Give me the application," I said.

At 4'9", I stood small but felt ten feet tall. My shadow stretched across his desk. He stared for a moment, then handed it over.

"Okay," he said. "I'll let you complete it. If you get at least two A's in the next two marking periods, we'll submit it—along with your writing award, band work, and science grades. But I don't think you—"

"Don't say it!" I cut him off. "I can do it—no thanks to you or my Grandma or any of y'all."

I stormed out, application in hand. Instead of going back to class like I'd promised Mr. Pahl I would, I went to the girls' bathroom, the same one where I'd first learned what womanhood meant.

I locked myself in a stall and cried. Punched the wall. Punched the door.

"God," I whispered, "what's wrong with me? Why doesn't anyone like me or believe in me?"

Silence.

But in that silence, something shifted. I stared at the application crumpled in my hand—the one Mr. Flood didn't think I could complete. The one with my name on it: Yolanda Washington.

Not Hoochy the troublemaker.

Not the girl who couldn't.

Yolanda.

Maybe God wasn't answering in words. Maybe he was answering with the paper in my hand. With the fact that I'd fought for it. With the fire that rose in me every time someone said, "you can't."

I wiped my face with the back of my hand and smoothed the application against my knee.

Then—a tap on the door. "Hoochy, you okay?"

I recognized the voice—my childhood friend Nish. I could see her pink shoes under the stall.

I unlocked the door. Nish stood there, her eyes soft with knowing. She didn't ask what happened. She just knew.

"I'm okay, Nish," I said, my voice steadier than I expected.

She told me her grandmother worked in the office with Mrs. Starr and was heading home for the day—her own story tangled in pain like mine.

"You gonna be alright?" she asked.

I looked down at the application again, then back at her. "Yeah," I said. "I'm gonna show them."

And I meant it. Not with anger this time—with something deeper. Something that felt like faith, even if I didn't have a name for it yet.

I Am Not My Grades.

The second semester came. Spring came with it.

My grades? Straight A's. Every class. I was finally ready to graduate.

"Grandma, can I get a dress for graduation?"

She lay on the couch—strange for her. Usually, she was on her feet, in the kitchen or posted by the door with a rolled-up scrub cap, no matter the season.

"What do you mean, a dress?" she said weakly.

"I need to dress up for graduation—it's not fair I don't have one!"

"Hoochy," she said, soft and tired, "go away. I don't feel like you today."

That stung.

"If it were Unk, you'd do it for him!" I yelled, stomping up the stairs. "I don't even want to go to graduation—and I don't want you there!"

I climbed out my favorite window—the one I used to talk to God from.

By then, I didn't go to church because Grandma made me. I went because I was trying to understand this God everyone said loved me—yet who seemed to only show me pain. Still, I went. I read my Bible. I talked to Him, not realizing those talks were prayers.

May turned to June. Graduation day arrived.

My sister Sheritta, pregnant with my first nephew, took me shopping for a dress. It was white, soft, and flowed at the bottom, with a V-neck that made me look grown—but not too grown. I even had four-inch white heels—something no one would let a fourteen-year-old wear today.

Sheritta did my makeup and hair. I looked in the mirror—and for the first time, I thought, I'm pretty.

They lined us up alphabetically. Of course, I was near the end—Washington. But I didn't care. I wanted to be the last name they called, to let it echo: "Yolanda Washington."

That name meant I had made it. I'd been accepted to Cass Tech—probationary, sure, but accepted. I was in the band, played two instruments, and volunteered at the summer festival program. I had learned to calm down—to find light instead of looking for trouble just to be seen.

No more fear of the dark. No more nightmares. No more silent tears from hands that used to creep in the night.

At the bottom of the stairs, waiting for my turn to be called, I searched the crowd.

Where is she?

She's coming.

I pictured her in that red hat, the red-and-gray-striped shirt, and red pants, the one nice outfit Grandma owned.

"Yolanda Washington!"

I stepped forward.

The crowd erupted, "Go Hoochy!" my classmates shouted. "That's my girl!" someone yelled from the back.

Feet stomped. Hands clapped. My name echoed through that auditorium like I'd won something bigger than a diploma.

And I had.

I had won against every "you can't" that ever tried to pin me down. Against the special ed label. Against Ms. Wells and her smirk. Against Mr. Flood's doubt. Against my own voice that whispered I wasn't good enough.

I walked across that stage in my white dress and four-inch heels, and for the first time in my life, I felt seen—not for the trouble I caused, but for what I'd overcome.

The principal handed me my diploma. I held it tightly.

Then I scanned the crowd. Where is she?

I searched the rows of faces—looking for that red hat, those red pants.

She wasn't there.

She's not coming.

My chest tightened. The noise around me dulled.

That old voice crept back in: *See?*

Anger: They still don't love you.

Me: I told her not to come.

Anger: You told her not to come, but she's the adult—and she listened anyway.

Me: I'm not alone—my classmates are here.

Anger: Yeah, with their family. You've always been alone, except for me. I'm here.

I kept scanning the audience. The ceremony was at the big church—Fellowship Baptist—behind the school. It reminded me of Shiloh Baptist Church.

Then the Caller repeated it, "YOLANDA WASHINGTON!" to get my attention.

The audience continued to shout, "Go Hoochy! Yeah, Hooch-Fat!" I stopped scamming the room and looked out at the people who were cheering for me.

Seeing all the ones who'd watched me come up—from that wild girl scribbling on bathroom walls, throwin' hands with the boys, bouncing around the classroom—to the one who just made it into Cass Tech.

They saw me, and maybe that had to be enough for now.

I lifted my diploma high above my head and straightened my shoulders. I let myself smile—not the practiced, polite smile, but a real one. A victorious one.

Because the truth was this:
I got straight A's.
I got accepted to Cass Tech.
I even received a summer job offer at St. Peter Claver right after graduation.

I had turned "I can't" into "I can," and no one could take that from me. Not even the empty seat where Grandma should've been.

And if she had been there to hear me say all this, she would've shaken her head and said, "I-I-I, I ought to poke you in the eye! It wasn't only you who did these things—but God!"

I walked off that stage holding my head high, even as my heart cracked a little. I had both things at once, the victory and the hurt. Faith and loneliness.

Maybe that's what growing up really meant.

I didn't know it then, but Grandma wasn't absent because of what I'd said. She was sick—sicker than I understood. Sicker than she'd let on. And she'd wanted to be there more than anything.

But I didn't know that yet.

All I knew was that I could.

And somehow, that was enough to carry me forward.

After graduation, I went home to 558 Eliot.

Grandma was still on the couch. She looked smaller somehow, like the illness was stealing pieces of her one day at a time. She'd stopped drinking—finally, after all those years—but her body was paying the price for all it had endured.

"How'd it go?" she asked, her voice barely above a whisper.

"Good," I said, standing in the doorway with my diploma in hand. "They called my name. Everyone clapped."

She nodded, her eyes closing for a moment. "I wanted to be there, Hoochy. I tried to get up, but..."

Her words trailed off, and I realized with a sick twist in my stomach that she had tried. She hadn't stayed home because I told her not to come; she stayed home because she couldn't.

The guilt hit me like a fist to the chest.

"It's okay, Grandma," I said quickly, moving closer. "You needed to rest."

But it wasn't okay. I'd spent the whole ceremony angry at her absence when I should've been worried, when I should've known.

She reached for my hand. Her grip was weak, but it was there.

"You did it, baby," she said. "I'm proud of you." Then she got real quiet, voice barely above a whisper: "Now all I need you to do is finish high school, Shanky." She drifted off and fell asleep.

"Grandma..." I started—wanted to let her know it was me, Hoochy—but her eyes were already shut, soft smile on her face. She was good. She was happy.

Those words, the ones I'd been waiting to hear my whole life, finally came. And they mattered. They mattered so much I almost couldn't breathe.

"Thank you," I whispered.

That summer, I prepared for Cass Tech. Probationary acceptance meant I had to prove myself all over again—but I was used to that. Used to being underestimated. Used to fighting for every inch of respect.

The Brewsters were still home. The only home I had. The red brick buildings still stood tall and stubborn. The courtyards still echoed with music, laughter, and pain. Grandma's house—558 Eliot—still smelled like fresh-dough biscuits on the mornings when she had the strength to bake.

I didn't know what the future would hold. I didn't know how long Grandma would be with me. I didn't know if Cass Tech would break me or build me.

But I knew this: I wasn't the same girl who played in the mud outside 657, waiting to be wanted.

I wasn't the same girl who cried in bathroom stalls, believing no one saw her.

I was Yolanda Washington. Hoochy. The girl who turned "I can't" into "I can." And somewhere between the grief and the grades, between the faith and the fear, I was learning that God's love didn't always look like I expected.

Sometimes it looked like a tap on a bathroom door.

Sometimes it looked like a classroom full of people shouting your name.

Sometimes it looked like a sick grandmother on a couch, whispering, "I'm proud of you." And sometimes—most times—it looked like the strength to keep going when every part of you wanted to quit.

Isaiah 41:10 still whispered in the back of my mind: Fear thou not; for I am with thee.

I was learning what that meant. Not that I wouldn't be afraid. Not that I wouldn't be alone sometimes.

But that even in fear, even in the loneliness, even in the one small home left in the Brewsters with my sick grandmother and my uncertain future, I wasn't walking by myself.

And that made all the difference.

Epilogue: On Better Days

AFTER IT ALL — THE WOMAN I BECAME FROM THE GIRL WHO SURVIVED

Everyone has their own take on anger, what it means, where it comes from, how to carry it. Some call it weakness, others strength. Some insist you bury it; others say unleash it without restraint.

But I've learned that anger, like any powerful emotion, is neither inherently good nor bad—it simply is. What matters is what we do with it—how we let it shape us, and whether we allow it to teach us or destroy us.

For years, I carried my anger like a stone in my chest— heavy, cold, unyielding. It was my childhood's companion, the shadow that followed me through adolescence, the weight I dragged into adulthood. I thought it was mine alone to bear—proof of my brokenness.

I didn't understand then that anger was trying to tell me something. Beneath its fierce armor was a child crying out to be heard, to be seen, to be valued.

The anger that grew me was born from pain and abandonment, from the confusion of a child trying to make sense of a senseless world. It was the rage of feeling invisible, of being left behind, of watching a mother choose her own demons over her children. But it was also something more than the fire that kept me alive when everything else tried to snuff me out. It was the voice that whispered, "You matter," even when no one else did.

Anger wasn't always my friend. Sometimes it consumed me, made me lash out, or stacked walls so high love couldn't climb them. There were moments when I became the very thing I feared—someone whose pain spilled over onto others.

Still, anger taught me resilience. It taught me I could survive what I never thought possible. It demanded I pay attention to my pain instead of burying it, that I honor my story instead of hiding it. In its own way, anger was the guardian of my truth.

The journey from that angry child to the woman I am today has been long and winding—full of setbacks, breakthroughs, and mercy I could never earn. I thought I'd never escape that rage. But slowly, painfully, I learned to transform it into understanding, compassion, and purpose.

Healing didn't mean forgetting. It meant acknowledging my wounds, feeling them fully, and choosing to move forward anyway. It meant recognizing that those who hurt me were often hurting themselves. That understanding didn't excuse their actions, but it freed me from being their prisoner.

My mother was broken long before she broke me. My father was gone long before he ever left. They did the best they could with what little they had, even if their best wasn't enough. I can hold both truths—that they failed me, and that they were human. That I deserved better, and they couldn't give it. That my anger was justified but carrying it forever would destroy me.

The anger that grew in me also had to be released—by me. Not all at once, that's not how healing works. But piece by piece, layer by layer, I learned to let it go. I realized that forgiveness doesn't mean forgetting or reconciling—it means loosening resentment's grip on your heart. It means choosing peace over war in your own soul.

And in that release, I found something unexpected—gratitude. Not for the pain itself, but for what it produced in me: empathy, compassion, and strength. The anger that grew me also grew my faith, my patience, and my ability to love fiercely. It made me a better parent, a better partner, a better human being.

Years later, I heard Dianne Reeves sing "Better Days" for the first time, and something in me went still. Her voice filled the room with questions I knew too well—questions about surviving the night, about holding on through the darkness, about whether morning would ever come.

And suddenly, I was back in my grandmother's living room—there she was in that red hat and red pants, her faith bigger than her frail body, her presence a sermon without words.

The song's questions were my questions: Will there be better days? Where does God live? Why won't He talk to me?

But unlike the song's story of a long night and a promised dawn, my own night stretched on for years. I was still bumping through the darkness, collecting bruises and wondering if the sun had forgotten me.

Then 1990 came. My son was born.

In his tiny face, I saw the answer I had been waiting for. He showed me that even in times of pain and uncertainty, faith shows up—in muscle memory, in God's track record, in those small breakthroughs that split the silence. The nights aren't always dark;

sometimes the moon slips through, stubborn and bright. Holding my son, I realized I was becoming someone else's better days—the dawn finally breaking after generations spent wandering through the night.

I leave these pages with gratitude—for the anger that protected me, for the pain that taught me compassion, for the silence that helped me hear God.

I'm grateful for my grandmother, who loved me when I was most unlovable. For every person who saw potential in me when I couldn't see it myself. For my children, who gave me a reason to heal and reminded me what unconditional love looks like.

I'm grateful for the hard lessons, the painful growth, the grace that showed up even when I didn't deserve it. For the strength I didn't know I had. For the woman who emerged from the wreckage.

To the angry child I was, thank you for surviving. Thank you for fighting. Thank you for refusing to give up. Because of you, I am here. Because of you, the cycle is broken.

And to you, the one reading this: Your anger is valid. Your pain is real. Your story matters.

The anger that grew within you was never meant to destroy you; it was meant to be your teacher.

Let it teach you and then let it rest.

Choose healing over hatred.

Choose growth over grudges.

Choose light, even when you still remember the dark. Morning will come. It may not look the way you imagined, but it will come.

And when it does, it won't erase the night—it will redeem it.

That's the promise my grandmother lived, the one Dianne Reeves sang, and the one I now carry in my own voice: "Morning don't come 'til you make it through the night."

I made it. And so will you.